gay city
volume 2

gay city
volume 2

2009

Edited by VINCENT KOVAR

Gay City Health Project
Seattle

GAY CITY: VOLUME 2
Copyright © 2009 by Gay City Health Project
Stories, artwork, poems and other contents © by their creators
Introduction copyright © 2009 by Vincent Kovar

First Edition

GAY CITY HEALTH PROJECT
511 E Pike Street
Seattle, WA 98122
www.GayCity.org

Cover art by jackson photografix

ISBN-10   144862214X
EAN-13   9781448622146

Printed in the United States of America
Set in Baskerville Old Face
Designed by Vincent Kovar

This book is for all
the artists and authors we've lost
&
for all those we've yet to discover
VINCENT
▼

CONTENTS

OUR SPONSORS

CULTURE
KING COUNTY PERCENT FOR ART

The Seattle Foundation
Your gift. Your community.

The Puffin Foundation Ltd.

ACKNOWLEDGMENTS

In addition to the fantastic sponsors and donors, several people were helpful in the creation of this book. The editor wishes to thank the staffs of Gay City Health Project, The Seattle Mayor's Office of Arts & Cultural Affairs, Richard Hugo House, Antioch University, 'mo Magazine, Seattle Public Libraries, 4Culture and the Virginia Kidd Agency, Inc. Thanks also to my parents, Kaladi Brothers Coffee, the Seattle Gay News, jackson photografix and to Mark Buchanan for use of his contact list..

A very special thank-you to Michael Wells of Bailey-Coy Books in Seattle for his ongoing and invaluable support of our community.

▼

INTRODUCTION

What qualifies something or someone as gay? In the past, this question was most often answered by listing what gay was not. Gay was not straight, not masculine and not desirable. In short, gay was not good.

Historically, the definitions and labels applied to the gay community were created by those outside of it. There were terms coined by clergy, psychologists and doctors, terms like deviant, urning, invert and homosexual. Of course, there were also the names of more pedestrian origins like nancy, faggot and queer.

I've always liked the term queer. It seems less like a synonym for undesirable and more like one for peculiar or unusually good. I imagine we could say it when traffic—which we expected to be impassible—suddenly clears up. How queer, we would say, and accelerate into the fast lane. A blind date might go queerly well. Our curmudgeonly boss might give us a raise. How queer.

As we've transitioned from being a sub-culture to a community, we've stopped calling ourselves queer or even gay. Instead, we've started using ever-lengthening acronyms in which we are assigned, not to a word, but merely to a single letter in a meaningless cluster of other letters. Will anyone ever look archly over the rim of a martini glass and state that this or that is so very LGBTQ? I doubt it.

I believe that as we become estranged from our language, we become alien to our own identity, a dangerous condition for those of an artistic bent. What is queerness really, but an identity? It is the act of being unusual and peculiar, two characteristics which are the very essence of an artist or a writer.

As gay people, we have transformed and retransformed ourselves. We have cried out to have our identity validated as something other than a neurosis. We've demanded—and sometimes gotten-- equal access to the institutions of justice, employment and marriage. We've gone from being a shunned sub-culture of sexual outsiders to a demographic that is courted by politicians and corporate marketers.

However, in this drive to convince the world that we are "normal" and just like everybody else, have we lost our fantastic, fabulous, blessed, joyous, delightful and sometimes shocking sense of being queer? Are we out-LOUD and out-PROUD or have we, as our more radical forbearers feared, merely and meekly assimilated? Does inclusion mean the end of our identity?

Mainstream society has ceased ignoring gays as a group but, maybe we've begun ignoring our own culture, our arts and our heritage; three tall pillars of identity. Consequently, it is now that we need a statement which expresses the uniqueness, even the deviancy of who we are. Gays are in desperate need of a manifesto.

A manifesto is an outcry that describes the direction, progress and energy of a people. Cultures have historically published these philosophical calls-to-arms as grand proclamations in the arts and in politics. Entire eras have been defined by their manifestos: surrealism, futurism, feminism, stuckism, punk. The U.S. published its manifesto as the *Declaration of Independence*. Marx shook the foundations of the world with his *Communist Manifesto*. Salvador Dali had his *Mystical Manifesto* and Ayn Rand opined in the *Romantic Manifesto*. Even Ron Paul summarized his 2008 Presidential Campaign in *The Revolution: A Manifesto*.

When I first published the call for *Gay City: Volume Two*, I asked for gay-themed works that were influenced by the artistic manifestos of the past. This did not go well. I received many emails either complaining about or questioning this decision. Yet, the work began to trickle in...slowly. A second call was published, this time asking, more explicitly, for work focused on themes of promises and commitments. After all, what is a manifesto, but a commitment to an identity and the implicit promise to remain true to its ideals?

At first, the pile of manuscripts, drawings and photographs on my desk depicted an identity in crisis, one that was unclear and in upheaval. It wasn't until I'd stepped back from this collection of highly individual pieces that I began to see the spirit of the whole. Everywhere, there are whispers of punk, of surrealism, and of any number of other manifestos. Yet, the work is not homogenous. The pieces do not assimilate into their neighbors. The contributors did not make a retrospective. Instead, they present ideas made different and made new. The work here could even be seen as a gay manifesto proclaiming the iconoclastic plurality of our identity. This is an anthology that looks up archly over its own pages and affirms that gays are indeed still fantastically, fabulously, blessedly, joyously, delightfully and sometimes shockingly queer.

Read on and see if you do not agree.

Vincent Kovar
June, 2009

MARC ACITO

Marc Acito's comic debut novel, How I Paid for College: A Novel of Sex, Theft, Friendship and Musical Theater won the Ken Kesey Award and made the American Library Association's Top Ten Teen Book List. It was also selected as an Editors' Choice by the New York Times and is translated into five languages the author cannot read. Its much-anticipated sequel, Attack of the Theater People, is now available. Tales of the City author Armistead Maupin called Attack of the Theater People "as sweet and nutty and irresistible as a bag of M&Ms."

For four years Acito shocked and amused readers with his syndicated humor column, "The Gospel According to Marc," which ran nationwide in nineteen alternative newspapers. He is now a regular commentator on National Public Radio's All Things Considered.

▼

DIAGNOSIS
by Marc Acito

A one, two, three,
I've got HIV,
A three, four, five
But I'm stayin' alive,
A five, six, seven,
Ain't ready for Heaven,
A seven, eight, nine,
'Cuz I'm feelin' fine.

WITH APOLOGIES TO EMILY DICKINSON
by Marc Acito

Because I could not stop for Death,
He kindly stopped for me.
And since I did not want to die,
I kicked him in the knee.
I boxed his ears, I punched his nose,
I smacked him in the head.
I whupped his sorry ass until
I knew that Death was dead.

BAD THEATER NIGHT
by Marc Acito

Friday's the night when my friends all impose
Invitations upon me to sit through their shows.
Overage ingenues, fat men in tights –
These are required for Bad Theater Nights.
Dancers who *jettae* their bodies through space
Regardless of rhythm, or tempo, or grace,
Gilbert and Sullivan time after time,
The Family Von Trapp with a mountain to climb,
Workshops in basements that leave me annoyed,
Musical tributes to Marx and to Freud,
Chekhov and Strindberg with many...a pause,
Avant-garde "happenings" that get no applause.

Week after week I see play after play,
And when they're all over, hell, what can I say?
I can't just say, hey, your performance was shit,
The scenery was awful, the show really bit,

I can't just say, hey, your performance was crap,
The fact that I sat through it makes me a sap

Or "Now that I've seen your performance as Puck
I've come to conclude that you really suck,"
Or, "Listen, I really don't want to offend,
But the best part was when the play came to an end."
No, even though they have just stunk up the place,
I venture backstage with a smile on my face.
I hug them and kiss them and that's the time when
I say to friends, "Well...you did it again!"

MY DATE WITH WALT WHITMAN
by Marc Acito

I thought that he'd be hot to trot
For all his sexy talk,
But then he grabbed me by the hand
And took me for a walk:
Past shipyards, houses, parks and squares,
An all-night pilgrimage,
"I won't get laid tonight," I thought
As we crossed the Brooklyn Bridge -
'Cuz Walt talked and talked and talked and talked
Of his Utopia
And everyone he's ever met;
Blah, blah, blah, blah, blah.
I know that he's some famous guy,
So I didn't interrupt,
But all night long all I can think
Is can't this man shut up?

ERIC ANDREWS-KATZ

Eric Andrews-Katz has been writing since he could hold a pen. He studied journalism and creative writing and then attended the Florida School of Massage. He has a successful Licensed Massage Practice and, with his partner Alan, calls Seattle home. His work can be found in Charmed Lives: Gay Spirit in Storytelling, The Best Date Ever and So Fey: Queer Fairy Fiction including his short story "Mr. Grimm's Faery Tale (nominated for the 2008 Spectrum Short fiction award). Eric is also a contributing writer for the Seattle Gay News. He can be found at: www.SeattleMassageGuy.com and reached at WriteOn530@gmail.com.

▼

NYC: 9-1-1
by Eric Andrews-Katz

For FTK

Greenwich Village
7:45 AM

Maria Concetti entered the apartment with the same comfort as if she were entering her own. Hearing a muffled voice from the back room she tried to be as quiet as possible, shutting the door and locking it behind her out of habit. She turned to find Daniel Wallace coming towards her, his finger still keeping place in the book in hand.

"Everything ok?" She quickly inquired. "I thought I heard voices."

"Couldn't sleep. Thought I'd read to him awhile; we're almost done." He held up a copy of *To Kill A Mockingbird.* "Always been his favorite."

Not knowing what to say, Maria held up the bag in her left hand. "I brought bagels." She tried to be cute; it came across as manic. Without waiting for a reply she turned to her right, took one step, and was at the counter of the small, city-life sized kitchenette. "How is he today?" She asked, putting the assorted selection on a plate and helping herself to what remained in the coffeepot.

"No change." Dan said sounding tired. "I just don't know if that's a good thing or a bad thing anymore."

"What about you?" Maria asked rejoining him in the cell-like foyer doubling as a dining room. Glancing over his face, she saw the dark lines under each eye. His stubble must have been at least two days old and while thinking about it, Maria couldn't remember the last time she saw the sparkle in the now faded hazel eyes. He looked years older than 34, the same age as she, and the thought brought her back with a shiver and a sip of coffee. "You don't look so hot."

Dan turned leading the way back through the shoebox apartment consisting of three rectangular rooms co-joined by open doorways. "I didn't sleep well. Kept waking up every half hour after 3. At 4:45, I just got up." They passed through the room Dan was sleeping in. It was originally a cozy television room but now it was bare; the Murphy bed closed within the wall. Only a table remained tucked in a corner and covered with an assortment of bottles to surrender willingly an array of medicinal remedies.

"I couldn't shake this feeling that something wasn't right." They walked to the back bedroom, pausing in the doorway. "I looked at Fredrick's vitals every hour, but everything checked out so..." He trailed off with a shrug.

Maria stepped close to Dan and wrapped her arms around his waist, careful with the coffee cup and resting her head on his shoulder. She tried to look past the assortment of machinery all keeping track of Fredrick's vital signs, and found it just as disturbing to focus on the figure resting in the makeshift, home hospital bed.

For a man of 37 years, Fredrick Klein looked ancient. The well-built body that once housed a vibrant life with an impish sense of humor lay quite still. His figure seemed depleted, his skin draped over each bone and an oxygen mask covered the lower half of his sunken face. Random movement under the closed lids allowed life to be detected, but the lids still remained closed without change for several days. A feeding tube was carefully inserted into one arm while a morphine IV drip fallaciously covered his pain with a peaceful mask. In the few moments of silence the secondary support reminded all of its presence with the start of the next mechanical whisper. Green and red flashes, not unlike Christmas lights, flickered back announcing the completion of the next breath cycle.

"He had a small coughing fit yesterday when Nikki was here around 6, but nothing too bad." He snorted a sharp laugh. "I was in the shower, but I think it freaked her out." He sighed wearily. "I checked the breathing tubes and gave him a little more morphine trying to make him as comfortable as possible. That's about all I can do. I'm restricted on how much I can give him at once and within a certain time frame" Dan reached back allowing his arm to cradle Maria's head. "For a moment I thought he might gain consciousness, maybe a furtive look or a fleeting glance. A wink was too much to hope for, I guess." His attempted forced laughter became a sharp barking.

"Anyone else been by?"

"Aside from the hospice workers and Nikki?" Dan counted on his fingers. "We've had Garth, Lynn, Mark, Fredrick's brother Bob, and Greg. So far."

"Must be hard to be well loved," Maria said with a small squeeze about Dan's waist.

"Yeah, but are they checking in on him, me, or their own conscious?"

"Dan!" Maria chided. "You have a good support system among your friends. They are your family. Both of you. They just want to help and say good bye."

"I know that and believe me I truly count my blessings, but with everyone trying to check in and say goodbye..." He didn't finish the sentence.

"What time does the hospice worker get here today?" Maria spoke softly in Dan's ear.

"Richard won't be here until 9:30."

"I have an idea." She leaned back and stepped around to face him. "Once he gets here, come out for an hour or so. The bagels will freeze and I'll take you out for breakfast and some real coffee."

"I don't know, Sweetie." He entered the bedroom and stepped over to his recently vacated chair. "The doctor said it would be 'soon', and I want to be here."

"He'll be watched and we'll just go down the street. You need to get out. It's been four days since you brought him home. I'm surprised you've taken the time away from his side to go to the bathroom."

"I used his bedpan once."

Maria gave her best friend a smile and put her coffee cup on the table between the chair and the bed. She faced Dan taking both hands in hers with a heavy sigh. "Half hour? When Richard gets here? Just a half hour?" Her request was rejected by the sorrowful conviction in Dan's expression. She closed her smile and tightened her lips in defeat. She exhaled loudly, her breath mixing with the pumping oxygen from the machine behind her. Maria looked from one of Dan's eyes to the other; her pleading blue orbs set and matched against his pained hazel shallow pools. *The* question repeated the stirring of doubt in her mind and she felt the need to revisit. Her strength renewed with a deep breath, Maria raised her smile along with a single eyebrow. "I have to ask you one last time."

"Again?" Dan said knowing what to expect from the tone in her voice. He let go of her hands retrieving his own coffee mug from the small bedside table. "You've had more 'one last times' than Cher."

"I know," said Maria, carefully placing a reassuring hand on his back. "But I have to ask anyway: Do you think Freddy could get better care in the hospital?"

Dan unsuccessfully blinked away a few tears as he looked over his life partner of nine years and carefully considered the question. His answer was reaffirmed momentarily and he wiped his eyes with his thumb and forefinger.

"No." The answer was simple and finite. His head began to rock back and forth as if confirming his decision. "After the last time when I almost lost him in July, he made me promise. He was very clear about it; he wanted to be home. This time I knew it was a matter of days and knew there weren't any options left. Now it's a matter of waiting for 'the sign'." Maria shook her head, questioning. "Fredrick told me that when it was time, he'd give me a sign."

"What kind of sign?"

"Who knows with him, he wasn't specific." Dan tried to unsuccessfully force a smile. "He said when he was ready he'd give me a sign. Knowing him it could be something as simple as my cell phone not working for 10 minutes or it could be as flashy as..." he paused to swallow the lump growing in his throat. "Fireworks in September."

Maria offered a smile knowing Fredrick's flair to capture attention. She rested her hand momentarily on Dan's shoulder before sliding it down his arm and taking his own in hers. "But maybe in a hospital, don't you think..."

"It doesn't matter what I think," he snapped, coming across harsher than intended. Immediately, he squeezed his friend's hand and tried to soften his tone. "This is about Freddy and what he wanted. Not about what I may or may not think is better. Always the control freak, he was very clear with his instructions."

Dan studied Maria's face. It was so full of compassion and concern that he almost felt the need to take care of her, to reassure her that everything would be all right. While being best friends for 12 years, she only got to know Fredrick for six; proper introductions made after Maria finally followed him to the city from Seattle. Dan could see the desire to help burning so fiercely within her and he could recognize the helpless inferno that held her in its control. He saw the pain she was feeling from the love she felt and for the first time he realized he was not alone in his grief.

Knowing his pain was shared among his friends was a double-edged sword. He felt the responsibility to diminish their discomfort and try to help ease their sorrows above his own. And Dan suddenly knew he didn't have the strength. There were two people here who needed him. If he tried to split his care into three parts, he would break; there would be no repair to his soul.

"I know you care," Dan said softly reaching out and hugging Maria tightly to him. "I know all of you care and more important, *he* knows you care." He felt her breathing become irregular and held her close. He rubbed his palm across her back until after a few sniffles she caught her breath and, patting his shoulder, signaled her release.

Maria pulled back without breaking contact. She studied Dan's eyes and saw a spark of the friend she fell in love with so many years ago.

"Fredrick has a lot friends who are here for him." She reached up to caress the back of his head resting her palm against his nape. "I want you to know that while I love Freddy, I'll let them take care of him." She gave Dan a quick peck and a brief hug before whispering in his ear: "I'm hear to take care of you." She kissed his neck and broke free so she could turn and wipe her eyes. "I'll tell you what," she offered glancing at her watch. "It's a little after 8:30 now, Richard won't be here for an hour." She took a deep breath giving her a final grounding. "Why don't I run out and do a little shopping for you; get some real food and definitely a pound of good coffee." She tried on a smile; it fit her well.

"Ok. Deal." He put out a hand for shaking. She took it pumping it slowly and shaking her head in rhythm.
"Fredrick is a lucky guy to have you. The world could end outside of this apartment and you wouldn't leave his side for anything. That's something to be envious of."

"My world is ending inside the apartment," Dan said quietly. "The outside can catch up."

"All right Sweetie but don't forget," Maria said hugging Dan's neck and kissing his cheek. "My niece is coming into town on Friday, and you said you'd take her to the lookout on top of the towers. I'm holding you to it." She smiled and blew him a kiss before walking towards the front door. Dan meandered behind her with an amused smile on his face. "I'm off shopping but when I get back," she squinted her eyes with a scrutinizing look and the hint of a smile that summoned memories of playful days of the past. "You're getting in the shower; you're smelling ripe."

Maria unlocked the door and pulled it open with fluidic motion. Half way out she paused to leave Dan with a comforting smile. Without a word, she waved her fingers in the air and continued letting the door close behind her.

Dan smiled as he locked the door and began to make his way to the back bedroom. Carefully walking around the prone figure, he touched each of the machines checking their digital and detached readings. Noting no changes, the emotional feeling of limbo reemerged, trapping and challenging him as to whether no change was good or not. He let go of his breath. Trying to wade in the pool of helplessness, Dan made his way back over to the bedside chair and table.

Dan picked up the book and began searching the last ten pages for his place. "Let's see," he said mumbling aloud. "Jem and Scout are coming home from the pageant; Jem's been attacked and someone brought him back to the house. Scout's told her version and ah," he said looking up at the unresponsive figure. "Here we are."

As Dan took a breath to begin reading, a siren started to wail outside quickly followed by another. When the two became an immediate symphony, Dan looked up at the window without having read a single word aloud.

"And I was really hoping to finish the book before she got back." Driven by curiosity Dan replaced the book on the tabletop and pulled himself out of the chair.

The wailing noise called him to the window like siren's song. Without knowing why, he hesitantly pressed himself against the windowpane and noticed a plume of blackened smoke rising in the distance. Fire trucks, ambulances and police cars raced down the adjoining major street all announcing their presence with ear shattering cries. He shifted his head noting the direction of the smoke. "Must be some fire though," he said resigning to not being able to see much more from his window. He turned away from the outside world and noticed Fredrick's eyes were open.

Dan's heart skipped several pulses as his brain tried to justify that Fredrick's eyes would close in a moment, but they didn't. His head remained turned towards him, and briefly Dan allowed himself to believe that Freddy might be able to actually see him. Without breaking eye contact, Dan cautiously moved over to the bedside. Reaching down he took his partner's hand and felt the weakened fingers brush against his palm. Dan's heart and breath stopped momentarily in unison. He tried to look passed the morphine glaze scanning Fredrick's brown eyes for any signs of their previous life and warmth.

A tear formed in the corner of Freddy's eye and Dan felt the breath being pulled from his own body. He squeezed his partner's hand and kicked off the slippers he was wearing. With mercurial grace Dan lowered the side of the hospital bed and slipped next to his husband. His arm moved around Fredrick's shoulders and Dan gently rearranged Freddy's head to lie on his chest. He ignored the feeling of cold tubes on his skin and let his fingers trace the small salt-and-pepper patch above his partner's right ear.

"Boo," Dan said softly, using the intimate nickname they kept for each other. He locked his focus on the wall directly in front of him never once allowing his fingers to stop their circular motion. "I love you and I know it's been hard for you, but it's ok I'm here." He swallowed a tightened grimace along with the lump in his throat. The outside consistent sounding of sirens blended into background noise and Dan was able to force it all away from him until silence emerged from his mind and cradled the two men together.

"You know you are well loved; not only by me but by our family, too. I know you are worried about me, but don't be; I'll be fine." He cradled his partner's head and ran his fingers along the jaw line. The stubble scratched his skin, but Dan took no notice. His fingers played with Freddy's earlobe before returning to trace the gray hairs through the fading brown ones. "And there are lots of people to look after me. We have good friends. So don't worry." He again swallowed hard. "You just rest now."

Dan barely got the sentence finished when he felt the final breath leave. His hands gripped tightly as if trying to hold back the life that slipped away and then he relaxed into quiet and calm pools of submission. The monotonous chime signaling the end of breath seemed comforting. It was a soothing red light that led Dan back from the darkness of possibilities and gently placed him within the comforts of reality, and Fredrick in his arms.

Without bothering to wipe away the subtle movement of tears down his face, Dan slipped out of bed and reverently rearranged Fredrick's arms to rest over his chest. He reached up and turned off the first of the alarming machines until only the consistent sounds of the sirens echoed somewhere from the far edges of the outside world. He walked around the bed and returned to the kitchenette with trancelike motion. His hand trembled as he reached for the wall phone and pressed the button for a dial tone.

When he heard nothing, Dan studied the keypad and pressed the green 'talk' button a second and then a third time. Feeling his jaw began to tremble he tightened it until his teeth were firmly clenched. He closed his eyes trying to find the last atoms of his patience and with a controlled inhale/exhale of breath, replaced the phone to its cradle and retrieved his cell phone from the table behind him to make the inevitable call to the authorities.

After several failed attempts with the second phone line, Dan began to understand. This was his sign. Fredrick was ready to leave and this was how he was letting Dan know.

Dan plugged the mobile phone back into its charger with the beginnings of a smile. He would wait the ten minutes out and then there would be time to call. In the meantime this was the sign as promised, and there was nothing to do but to acknowledge it. He kept his word and Fredrick was rewarding him with ten minutes of time to gather himself together. The day would be unending, but for now Dan had ten minutes of solitude and that was time enough.

A feeling of comfort crept through the numbed veins of Dan's body as he mechanically walked to the back bedroom. He sat down and picked up his book thumping through the pages until he began to read aloud:

" 'His lips parted into a timid smile, and our neighbor's image blurred with my sudden tears.
'Hey, Boo,' I said."

Dan stopped reading. His voice fell and cracked open. From the rubble, a sound erupted. Slowly it crept into a howl and ripped through the ceiling of the building. The cry mixed with the black haze gathering in the sky and there found company in the presence of a million others.

JEFFERY BEAM

*Jeffery Beam's award-winning works include Beautiful Tendons,
Visions of Dame Kind, Fountain, and the Audie Award-winning
spoken word/multimedia What We Have Lost. Gospel Earth
(England) and Invocation, are due in 2009. Life of the Bee, with
composer Lee Hoiby, continues to be performed on the
international stage. The Carnegie premiere can be heard on Albany
Record's New Growth. In 2008, Submergences appeared in the
surrealist anthology Madder Love, and in Boston composer Steven
Serpa premiered Heaven's Birds a cantata for World AIDS Day
based on three poems from The Tendons. Beam is poetry editor of
Oyster Boy Review. www.unc.edu/~jeffbeam/index.html*

▼

* "Self Portrait" and "In a Far Country" originally appeared in The Beautiful Tendons: Uncollected Queer Poems 1969 – 2007 (White Crane Wisdom Series, 2008). "Posession Sutra" will appear in my next book Gospel Earth due in 2010 from Skysill Press, England. "Oh, and I Thought" appears in a book seeking a publisher, The Broken Flower and other poems.

OH, AND I THOUGHT
by Jeffery Beam

1.

Oh, and I thought I was special.
It's a game we humans play
to attract your attention. We
think that persistence in
believing it is all for us, separately,
will make you come down, cover us like
snow, each chosen, quietly, before the
doom
of Death, that close darkness,
takes us up, and Death instead
will be white shadows, and
cold, simple, silence. Instead,
we are meant to learn its
opposite. All together we are
special, but separately, never.
Spokes in an eternal wheel.

2.

I lied before when I said
separately we're not special.
A half-truth at least. Both,
neither/and, we are conflict
impossible to define without
exaggeration or egotism.
In and out of the world
our roles differ, but when
in the world most fully, but
simultaneously, aside, a vibration
begins. A tree bends. The
wind through our branches.
Then. That's the special time.

SELF-PORTRAIT
by Jeffery Beam

1

I drew it
coarse
I drew it with a lean
toward something
cross

I struck it with an antler
and a tail

I brushed it fine
then began
the spell

This image wiry
faintly huge
emblematic
strange

evokes the falling timber
round the house

In the fireplace
on the panel
two bonfires roar

I give them
each
a portion
of my heart

2

I think it odd
almond eyes
gleaming

Turn to take the kettle from the fire
A tea-cup full

A yellow-flash
The lamp and my throat
shudder

3

By morning
it has spoken
black and whistling

A strange hand
takes pen

I name you friend

POSSESSION SUTRA
by Jeffery Beam

I knock at
the door

No one answers

I knock at the door
again

No one comes

No one comes
I ask
      Who are you

I am no one
Who are you

Then
No body

IN A FAR COUNTRY
by Jeffery Beam

1

Let your hair
barely bronze
naked
tattoo in scarlet the marks
where the act
the touch

Beauty
The link
between
the cabinet of your body

2

Nights
lonely men festooned with red
Chinese lanterns
expose themselves

White bed sheets atop the grass

3

The laid-back mover

We were on the move
Visible
his hands
slowly urging it faster and

more

4

Me against the pre-dawn
The shadow

A rhinoceros horn
of angels

5

When the luggage was opened and
they had apparently
bedded the
romance

his skin
vanilla-colored

JAY BEE

"Playful living at every naked moment possible." My photography seeks out the brilliance in simplicity. By spending time with my subject, I know the precise moment to click the shutter and capture "your" essence. What results is my subject at their natural best. I am constantly inspired by others' delight and smiles as they engage with my images.

▼

SAVING YOUR DAY
by Jay Bee

In Due Time
by Jay Bee

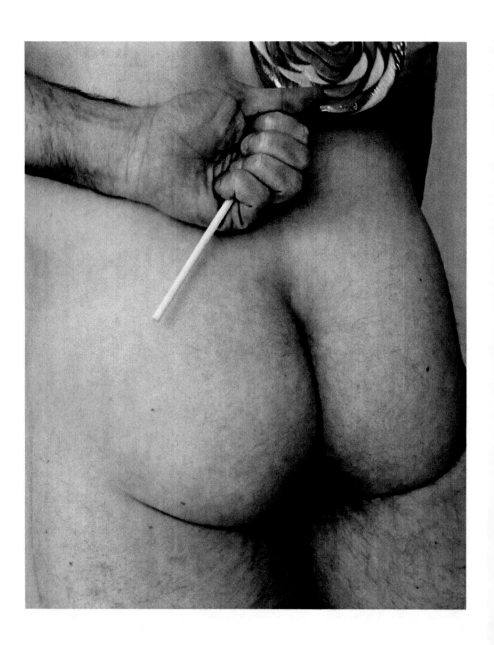

AHIMSA TIMOTEO BODHRÁN

Ahimsa Timoteo Bodhrán is the author of Antes y después del Bronx: Lenapehoking, winner of the Fall 2008 New American Press Chapbook Contest. His award-winning poetry and nonfiction appear in over a hundred publications in eleven nations. A Ph.D. candidate in American Studies at Michigan State University, he is the recipient of Dean's Recruitment, Interdisciplinary Inquiry and Teaching, and Dissertation Completion Fellowships and a Somers Excellence in Teaching Award. He is currently completing Yerbabuena/Mala yerba, All My Roots Need Rain: mixed blood poetry & prose and Heart of the Nation: Indigenous Womanisms, Queer People of Color, and Native Sovereignties.
http://www.msu.edu/~bodhran

▼

AMERIKKKA THE BEAUTIFUL
by Ahimsa Timoteo Bodhrán

for Barbara Smith, Marcus Kuiland-Nazario,
& the brother/sisters of Days of Pentecost

O Beautiful for Gracious Skies
For Amber Waves of Grain

sometimes i do not feel safe in Amerikkka
sometimes i do <u>not</u> feel safe in Amerikkka

comin home from the movies   i bump inta
a friend   he is mixed like me   a queer colored boy
a friend   n i breathe easy   easier   i am home

comin home from the movies   i bump inta a friend
a queer colored boy   mixed like me   n i realize
after having sat thru a movie
a black n latino drag movie
 that he is home ta me
  that all my colored boyz n girlz r home
   that often we r the only home we have

sat thru this movie deep n painful
sometimes funny but only
sometimes
it wuz serious
 serious as slavery
 serious as a gay black drag queen killing a straight whiteboy
  by steppin on him
   his/her heel going thru the whiteboy's forehead
   killing him
   instantly

For Purple Mountains' Majesty
Above the Fruited Plain

the white people in the audience
they laughed at this
    laughed as my brother/sister killed this whiteboy
    he/she saying it wuz for four hundred years of oppression
       how the white people laughed at this
       they being the majority in the theatre
       este teatro en el centro de la misión
       they laughed all the way thru the movie
       times when i wuz   clutchin myself
               twisting inside
            straight face outside
         no sign of humor
          motherfuckin white people
       laughed all the way thru the movie

i know
amos n andy
chico n the man
tonto n lone ranger
all trained u real well
but   we r not cartoons
       we r not some cosby comedy
       u can turn off n on with a remote
                        our pain is real
       four hundred plus years of oppression is real

comin home on the bus from the movies
i grab on ta my brother n   hold him
                  tell him   what has happened
                  he nods   knowingly

i pull the cord   get off the bus n
   pull out my keys
      put them between my fingers
         like blades
            like my momma taught me how
            like she knew i would

i gotta go home now but
i don't wanna cut up my
                   three
                    white
                      roommates

Amerikkka Amerikkka
God Shed His Grace on Thee

motherfuckers still can't get my name right
showed my bi white roommate a poem today
written just like the one i'm readin tonite
n she said it   sounded like a child
            sounded like a child's voice
        cuz it wuzn't written in
      "standard
      english"
jump off the damn bus n
   pull out my keys
      put them between my fingers
         like blades
            like my momma taught me how
            like she knew i would

i gotta go home now but
i don't wanna cut up my
                   three
                    white
                      roommates

just want them ta fuckin leave
just want y'all ta leave
just leave my people b
we don't want no trouble
we just wanna go home now
i just wanna go home now
but sometimes u just ain't got no home
in Amerikkka
n that ain't no joke so
don't u dare fuckin laugh
don't u dare fuckin laugh

And Crowned Thy Good
With Brotherhood
From Sea to Shining Sea

BRIAN BROWN

Brian Brown is a historian and photographer in Fitzgerald, Georgia. His illustrated history, Georgia in the Great Depression, is forthcoming from Arcadia Publishers. Poetry recently appears or is forthcoming in Chiron Review, Town Creek Poetry, Louisiana Review, Velvet Mafia and Vain, among others. His images of the endangered vernacular architecture and cultural iconography of the Wiregrass Region may be seen at vanishingsouthgeorgia.wordpress.com

▼

MIDLIFE CRISIS
by Brian Brown

The changing smell of his deodorant
first roused suspicion, then regret,

at the passing of another memory,
a familiar sensual landmark

lost to time. Damn middle age
her heartless handmaidens.

You try to remember his theme song,
tap it out with your foot

while you wait to pick him up
for a night out in the clubs,

but too many others have come and gone
since you broke up.

He peeks out the window
as you pull into his driveway,

and he's already chugged two beers,
done poppers to ready himself.

You know this game too well,
already wanting it to end,

until he introduces you to the boy
he met online, reassures you

he's versatile, he'll do anything.

HOPE IN THE DUST
by Brian Brown

Hope then was a humid swamp, all tangled.
Stuck together like an old *Honcho*
my parents found beneath my bed
five years after I moved out, on with my life.

I had left a smothering bedroom
shared with my brother into puberty,
my blended cotton sheets an unkind temple
hiding the emerging spectrum of my desire.

When I finally got him, really got him,
imagined man of dreams in steel-toes,
he took my like a schoolboy
behind the woodshed, made me
scream for Jesus over the neighbors' sleep.

And the only consolation I got was a snub
as we passed on Central Avenue,
epithets of faggot and cocksucker
echoing like a migraine all over town.

Hope now is that bastard left standing
alone in the dust, on the broken road to bliss.
Another notch on my belt
as I lay down to memory his every thrust.

NEW RELIGION
by Brian Brown

This latest quest for enlightenment
finds me reinventing the past,
recalling my first good fucking
through Billy's ultramarine eyes.

My knees were torn and bloody,
a perverse stigmata on cheap carpet,
first time so sore
as I was forced to abdicate
all my old beliefs
to the deification of his flesh.

His thrusts funneled me helpless
through a river of lava,
oozing like forbidden doctrine
over the weathered dunes,
tattooed gospel of his stomach.

How he sat naked on the red sofa
in the cautious glow of morning,
rolled jailhouse cigarettes,
cadged leftover liquor from plastic cups,
while I pretended to sleep.

His soft glow became the room,
and in time the words
to beautiful psalms,
long committed to memory.

MICHAEL CAROSONE

With his partner, Joseph LoGiudice, Michael Carosone is writing and editing a collection of essays on the lives of Gay Italian American men. Michael is in search of a publisher to publish his first book of poetry. He is beginning to write his memoir. He wishes to publish his essay on the marginalization of Italian American writers and Italian American literature. He wishes to continue to write on marginalized peoples and literatures, especially Italian Americans and people of the Gay, Lesbian, Bisexual, Transgender, and Queer (GLBTQ) Community. At various conferences, he has presented papers on Queer Italian Americans.

▼

BACK
by Michael Carosone

forward
they need to face forward
they need to face the facts
we gays are not going back in the closets
the same way that
blacks are not going to the back of the buses
the same way that
women are not going back in the kitchens

forward
they need to face forward
they need to face the facts
otherwise they can go
back
back
to where they belong
Back!

GAY 101
by Michael Carosone

Dear Suicide Attempt,

You
wrote
me
to ask
for
role models.

Here is a short list.

(this will keep you busy for awhile)

Consider
it a Gay 101:

(the names are in alphabetical order,
not in order of importance,
for they are all important)

Kate Bornstein
Barbara Gittings
Frank Kameny
Larry Kramer
Audra Lorde
Harvey Milk
Vito Russo
Bayard Rustin
Alan Turing
Virginia Woolf

Sincerely,
Your Gay Role Model

P.S.: you can always Google: "gay"

WEDDING
by Michael Carosone

Ironically,
it was at her wedding
where she introduced
him
as
my
friend.

But,
what does she care.
She is allowed
to marry.
I'm not.

MY LAUNDROMAT
by Michael Carosone

I will buy a Laundromat
so that
I can take the perfectly blue and green
rounded sphere which we call planet Earth
and give it a very needed cleaning.

I would love to wash the Chinese out
of Tibet, and all the other bully nations
that don't belong. Those countries that think
they are better. Those countries that need
to feel superior. Those countries that
rape and ruin others. You know, "those" countries...

I would not use chlorine bleach.
I don't want every thing to turn white.
Colors must be preserved.
I would wash inside out so that the
colors do not fade, and if they happen
to run, then, that's okay.
Maybe, I will not separate.
Maybe, to save some money on the machines.
Maybe, to have peace.

Or, maybe, I will separate, but for no other
reason than wanting my white underwear
to remain white and not pink from
the dye of my red T-shirt.

I will clean the minds.

I will wash the emptiness from the
stomachs of starving children, and
hope that the suds fill them.
Turn the knob for eight cycles--
for an eight course meal.

I will wash in much needed education,
and dry out too much ignorance.
A fluffy, dryer sheet will read:
"Thanks to ALL of the Teachers."
Fold in college degrees and jobs
for all. Get rid of wrinkled
unemployment lines, and soup lines at shelters.

Remove the starch from the Republicans.
Add some to the Democrats.
I will wash the Right-winged, Bible-thumping,
fake-Christian, Conservative Politicians out of

Women's bodies, and dry them in hell.
I will use the spin cycle to spin a woman
all the way to the White House.
(And NOT as First Lady.)
I will wash the eyes of the people in
other countries so that they will see
our Female Leader, and elect their own.
I will wash clean the eyes of the people in
this country so that they will never again
see the darkness.

I will clean minds.
I will open minds.

I will NEVER use detergents filled with
chemicals which were tested on animals for the
safety of humans: pouring the skin
off of cats and dogs, pouring the blood
from the veins of mice, pouring
the sight from rabbits. Pouring out life.
Detergents that clean in the moment
but destroy in the future. Detergents
that wash away the blue and green
of our perfectly rounded sphere.

Mother, I will wash and dry and fold you
just right. I will clean away those
who wish to hurt you.
I will wash you again and again and again.

I will wash in a lot of love.
And dry out all of the hate.
And with the natural soaps, I will add
kindness and honesty. Take out greed.
Cruelty does not survive in the cleanliness
of hot, cold, and warm waters. I will
drown out the sounds of nonsense,
allowing some silence to rotate as the
washer whirls and the dryer tumbles.
The machines are loud enough.

I will clean the minds.
I will clean the hearts and souls.

I will wash away the boredom on the faces
of children, teenagers, and adults.
Pre-treat with happiness.
Fold with happiness. Hang with happiness.
Wear happiness on the sleeve.
Stop yearning for what we do not have.
Satisfy with a simple scent. Every thing
shrinks. Every thing dies. Love what we have.

I must remember that drying shrinks.
Forget dry-cleaning. I'd rather wash and dry.
I must remember to add a new way
of raising boys and girls in with the laundry.
Make the dirty clothes clean again.
Definitely, wash away violence.

I will buy a Laundromat
so that...

VINCENT DIAMOND

Vincent Diamond's short story collection, Rough Cut: Vincent Diamond Collected was published by Lethe Press in 2008, and has stories in Best Gay Erotica 2009, Country Boys, Truckers, Men of Mystery, Best Gay Romance 2007, Hot Cops, Love in a Lock-Up, Best Gay Love Stories 2005 and 2006, in various e-books from Torquere Press, and online at Fishnet, Clean Sheets and Ruthie's Club. Time away from the keyboard is spent in the dressage ring, picking up the correct diagonal at the trot. Free stories, excerpts, and more info is at: www.vincentdiamond.com.

▼

Not To Forget
by Vincent Diamond

A cool April morning with that distinctive Florida dampness in the air. Chunky hip-hop beats pulsed from a neon-green Acura waiting at the stoplight. Russo Vasquez had all the bay doors open to his shop, plus the entry door into the customer sales area. He yelled over the stuttering buzz of the power wrench. "Marcos! Telefono!"

Marcos Moretto set down the tool with care on the workbench. He always did, like he knew that tools were expensive. It was something Russo had noticed the first week Marcos started work in the garage. Unusual for a parolee three months out of Raiford. His shaved-bald head gleamed with fine sweat. Circled around each of his meaty biceps, barbed wire--done in prison-blue ink, and on his left hand, a small crimson heart.

Russo moved back to his cash register. At age seventy, he was too old to do much more; he could hardly raise his arthritic arms overhead to do simple oil changes. No matter, he had the boys around for that: his two grandsons, Angel, and now, Marcos. Snatches of his conversation drifted into the open door leading from the work bays.

"... my paycheck. ... deposit it in the ATM ... get two hundred back...."

"... yeah, after lunch. ...be here late. We got two radiator pulls to do..." Russo heard the phone click down, saw Marcos head back to the Ford he'd been working on. Mrs. Soljarero came in, chattering away, and the uniform delivery came, and the Pepsi vendor. Russo thought nothing more about it until the gringo showed up.

Vasquez's garage was located deep in the heart of Hispanic Tampa, bordered by Armenia Avenue on the west and Cypress Street to the south. Whites who came in were usually lost and on-edge; their eyes were a little too wide, their words a little too polite. This one was different though, he had more confidence. Russo saw him walk in but didn't look up from his crossword puzzle.

"Mr. Vasquez?" The tall, blond man stood in his shop, lanky in his suit pants, creased and sharp.

Russo noticed the crisp tailored shirt and shiny tie; they looked expensive. "Si, hoy Vasquez. Que?"

The Spanish didn't put off the gringo. He replied in Spanish himself, though the syllables were a little stiff. "Estoy buscando a Marcos."

Looking for Marcos? A bill collector? Parole officer—maybe. This one was so clean-cut that Russo's suspicions were pinged. Marcos had been working for him for nearly three months but he'd never had any visitors at the shop. He punched in, humped on cars all day, ate out back with the guys but--never really said much. Quiet. Quiet in a dark way, like a man who'd been through bad times. Russo recognized the signs: the hooded eyes hiding something, the squared off shoulders always tight. Russo had seen that in his own mirror, long ago.

"Maybe he here, maybe he not. Depends." Russo was protective of his crew, always had been. Sure, they got into trouble sometimes, did stupid things, usually involving alcohol, but they were good boys, all around. Plus, Marcos was older than the others so Russo didn't think Marcos would do anything stupid ... Still, this strange man was here.

"Tyler!" Marcos stood framed in the doorway, a tire looped in one elbow. His smile was open and easy.

"Hey, Marcos." Tyler reached out with one hand, then stopped and smoothed down his tie.

"Be right there. Mr. V, okay to take a break?" Marcos waited for Russo's reply. Not that it mattered, as if anyone could make bull-sized Marcos work when he didn't want to. Still, it was a respectful gesture, a nod to the senior man.

"Sure, that's fine. You take a break, talk to your friend, si?" "I'm gonna wash up. Meet you in back." Marcos went to the utility sink in one corner and scrubbed down his hands and arms. To Russo's surprise, he even bent over and soaped off his face.

Russo led Tyler through the garage to the round picnic table and curved benches set up behind the shop. A lone Florida holly leaned over the table, sending fingers of shade over the scuffed redwood. The shabby umbrella overhead snapped in the April breeze. The homey smell of arroz con pollo drifted from the Cuban restaurant two doors down.

"Nice to meet you finally, Mr. Vasquez." Tyler held out one hand. "Marcos speaks highly of you. I'm Tyler Tanner."

Russo's ears were used to more florid tones and heated talk; the flat American accent sounded pale, dull even. He shook Tyler's hand. "Glad to meet you."

The gringo was even-featured, handsome in a California surfer kind of way. Russo knew that his granddaughters would swoon over this one, tall and blond and blue-eyed. And dressed so fancy. This man used his brain to earn his money, not his hands.

Americano muy lindo.

Marcos strode towards them, a bottled iced-tea in his hand, its turquoise label shining. He'd taken off his dirty uniform shirt and his white tank top gleamed in the spring sun. Russo edged away.

In the shadow of the work bays, Russo hovered over Angel, who swore as he tugged on a too-tight fan belt. Angel kept up a running commentary on *everything,* all day long, so he didn't notice that Russo only watched the men outside in the sunshine. Curious.

Russo saw Tyler straddle one of the benches, facing Marcos. The bald man tugged his paycheck from a pocket; Russo recognized the bright yellow paper he'd signed that morning. Marcos penned on its back and handed it to Tyler. The breeze pushed over little bits of their conversation.

"... get those textbooks and we'll..."

Tyler folded the check and slipped in his shirt pocket. He leaned forward, elbows on his knees. Marcos's head tilted once in a while and Russo caught a flash of his bright smile in the sunlight. Tyler traced one finger around the iced tea's rim.

"...do about dinner..."

He like this man, feels easy with him.

Russo stretched his back and sighed. Angel pulled him down to the back of the sedan and bitched about the drum rotors. When he looked again, Marcos and Tyler had moved over to a zippy orange Mustang, Tyler's he assumed. It was snugged up next to Marcos's old Chevy SS.

They both stood with their hands pillowed behind their backs, leaning against the car. Tyler laughed and jostled one shoulder against Marcos. The warm breeze ruffled up Tyler's hair, like a halo around his smooth face.

A car alarm zinged off at the front of the shop; Russo had to check on it. When he looked back, Marcos leaned over the Mustang's driver's side, one caramel-skinned forearm on the roof.

When Marcos came back into the shop, his step was light, his shoulders loose and relaxed.

Just before seven o'clock, Russo locked his office door and noticed the shop light still on in the bays. Marcos was at the workbench, turning rotors.

"Whatchoo doing, Marcos? It's payday. It's late! Go home."

"Just wanted to get these turned. Angel needs them for the Chevy first thing on Monday."

"Why didn't Angel turn the damn rotors himself? Never mind, silly question." Russo leaned against the workbench. The wood vibrated against his back as the drum rotor machine shrieked.

"I don't mind, boss. This is a good customer; she takes care of her car." Marcos kept working, his thick fingers dirty and oily. Russo could smell the acrid garage on him; after thirty years of grease and oil on his own skin, he recognized that it would never go away.

"Your boy, Tyler, he's special, no?"

Marcos glanced up at him then focused on the rotors again. "Yeah, he's a good guy."

"He dress mighty nice, what does he do?"

"He's a security consultant."

"Security? He sell like Brinks and stuff?"

Marcos snickered a little. "No, corporate security, a little more involved than burglar alarms. He's in school for a Systems degree." The squeal of the metal was loud in the quiet garage. The bay doors were closed and outside, Friday night traffic had lightened.

"Ah, a smart man." Russo watched the street but he could see Marcos from the corner of his eye. He sighed and wiped his face. "You listen to an old man tonight, yes, someone who has smarts, maybe in a different way?"

Marcos stopped working and gazed at him, eyes direct but questioning. "Yes, sir." He turned off the grinding machine and it whined down into silence.

Always respectful this one. If only my own grandsons were so. "I seen some bad times. I think you seen some bad times too."

Marcos crossed his arms, his biceps solid and thick. He turned and faced the street as well. Russo saw their reflections in the door's glass, an old man bent and soft and a young man, standing straight and strong. But hurting.

Russo went on. "So, let me tell you a few things. Your family come from Cuba, too? Si, I thought so. When Castro take over, he do terrible things to his people. My uncle, my father and I went into one of the work camps, that's what they called them but we weren't doing no stinking work. We were rotting."

In the glass, Marcos's eyes held him. He wasn't listening to be polite or to placate the boss; he was really listening, Russo sensed it.

"I get out, the others don't. And I try hard to forget, very hard. But I never did. And it burned at me, made me angry, made me an ugly man. Until Essy. My Esmerelda, God rest her soul." Russo made the sign of the cross, kissed his fingers. "We together for forty years. Course, times have changed. I would not be allowed to marry a sixteen-year old girl, nowadays, they would throw me in jail. But, we have good years together."

Russo felt his breath hitch. Two years dead and she could still make him feel weepy.

"She was fifty-six when she died. The hardest day of my life. Thing is, Marcos, she don't help me to forget; she helped me to remember. To remember that people could be good and kind and sweet; she had that and she gave some to me."

Marcos stood absolutely still.

Russo puffed out his cheeks. "So, I don't know what bad times you have had; I don't need to know. But, I am thinking that this Tyler, he help you remember, maybe."

Marcos lowered his head. Russo saw his fingers tighten over his forearms.

"The best day of my life was the day I put my ring on her finger. That's all I'm gonna say." Russo patted Marcos's arm, quick and light. He shuffled to the front door. "You go to- you go home now, Marcos. Leave the rotors, I mean it."

Marcos looked up at him finally. His brown eyes were soft in the dim light, gentle now. "Thank you, Mr. V."

Russo smiled. "Go home."

TYLER DORCHESTER

Since 2005, Tyler Dorchester has based The Brotherhood on his nearest and dearest, a collection of cage-rattlers, shit-disturbers, deep-thinkers, and how-life-is unravellers. Dorchester himself is completely covered in a pelt of soft fur, as he suffers from hypertrichosis, or "werewolf syndrome". Though he shaves his entire body, he is revered as a god in the bear community. Dorchester is also VERY tall, and a total top. His strip has been published in a collection, and can be found in Vancouver's and Toronto's Xtra. The Brotherhood's further adventures can be found at www.Brotherhoodworld.com. ▾

MY BACK
by Tyler Dorchester

CREEP IN THE NIGHT
by Tyler Dorchester

DREAMS OF 2.5 CHILDREN
by Tyler Dorchester

iPHONE
by Tyler Dorchester

INTRODUCING DOVE
by Tyler Dorchester

BOOT TO THE HEAD
by Tyler Dorchester

MATISSE FLETCHER

Matisse Fletcher is a member of MPowerment Core Team through Lifelong AIDS Alliance. This is her first time being featured in the Anthology.

▼

WEDDING VOWS
by Matisse Fletcher

He felt like some housewife whose husband was about to leave for war in a distant country. Though instead of a sundress and pearls, he wore socks. And that was about it. For some reason, it made things worse hearing the words while he was naked.

Edward was fully dressed, and had a suitcase in his right hand. The door was open, and Mrs. Alcott--the nosy woman across the hall-- had already found an excuse to wander by and peek in. Seeing Daniel standing naked in the middle of the comfortably large living room sent Mrs. Alcott scuttling away in titters and a gleeful outcry of "Oh, my!" Daniel could picture her making the rounds to all her gossipy friends. He sat down hard, right on the floor.

"Will you please not do that?" Edward's hand, poised on the doorknob, gently slipped away and fell to his side.

"What more do you want?"

"I was hoping you wouldn't-"

Daniel stared hard at the floor and interrupted his partner of four years, "You were planning on sneaking out. Without a word."

"Maybe because I knew you'd act like this," he snapped, groaning at the glare Daniel shot him. "We could have talked once you calmed down."

"Why are you doing this to me?"

Sitting sliding down the wall, Edward sat, one knee crooked up for his elbow to rest on. "It's what *you* did to *us*."

A coil of cold fear tightened at the base of his spine. Daniel wished desperately he had more clothes on. "How did you know?" he whispered, eyes looking anywhere but at Edward. He'd been *so* careful, especially after Edward had threatened to leave the first time.

Pushing the door closed with his elbow, he leaned his head back against the doorjamb, snorting derisively. "How could you think I wouldn't notice? People say love is blind. Not this. Not after four years of this. This kind of love opens your eyes." Rain pattered against the large window overlooking Cal Anderson Park. "Especially when that love is using-"

"I'll stop," he whispered, "This time, I'll stop."

"This time? No. Maybe when I'm gone you'll finally choose what you care more about." He swallowed hard. His eyes stung.

His mouth felt impossibly dry. Helplessly Daniel waved his hand, motioning around the condo. "Look what we have together. I'm not some tweaked junky, Ed. I make six figures. We have a retirement plan. I pay for this big place, this beautiful view."

"Doesn't matter how big this place is. Three's still a crowd," he said. "And don't hold your salary over me. I have my own savings, aside from the joint account. I can make it fine on my own." Standing again, Edward looked hard at Daniel. "I love you enough to do this. The first time we worked through this I thought that was it, with all the family and friends who came for your intervention. We were all there to support you. But not me, not this time. It's my life too, and your drugs are infecting every part of it."

Suddenly Daniel was up on his feet, feeling dizzy. In the bathroom lay the needle and the tourniquet. And the... He was about to take a hit when he noticed that Edward's toothbrush and razor were gone. That sinking realization took away the itch for a hit, but now it was creeping back as a storm of emotions raged through him. Sweat trickled down his back. He hadn't used since last night, while Daniel was asleep.

"So you're going back on your vows?" Daniel was breathing hard, nearly panting. "When you said, 'Through sickness and in health?'"

"Not sickness that you inject into yourself."

In place of fear began to develop anger. Daniel ran a hand through his hair. "It's not like I'm injecting it into you. I can make sure it doesn't affect you. I'll slow down, okay? For you, I'll slow down, and then I can stop after that."

"For me?" Edward slammed a fist into the wall, his entire arm seizing up with the pain. In seconds his face was streaked with tears. "Do you know what you did for me?" He attacked the buttons on his shirt with uneasy fingers, ripping each free and breaking more than a few completely. Next he tore it off entirely, holding out his arms for Daniel to see all of his upper body.

The silence that followed was long and heavy. Daniel stared at the finger-shaped bruises lining Edward's hips and neck. Struggling to remember, he closed his eyes. Last night he'd taken a big draw. He'd had an important pitch that day for one of his company's most promising clients, and it hadn't gone as well as planned. Seems like none of them had been going well lately. His supervisor told him the next one could be his last. That's why he needed it so bad last night. But what happened after?

"There was another part of those vows," he said. "Some bullshit about honoring and cherishing." Gripping himself tightly, he glared at Daniel. "Last night," he stopped, faltering. "Waking me up like that. You didn't even hear me when I told you to stop. And you were too out of it to even use a condom. I'm going to get tested. I'll let you know if you gave me anything," he spat, grabbing his suitcase and swinging it up with him to go through the door.

"Ed!" He grabbed his partner's arm. "Don't leave, you don't even have a shirt on. Wait, please. I'll stop. I never meant to hurt you, ever. I didn't know what I was doing. I'll stop. Please, I'll stop." Now he was crying, even though his body felt there was nothing there to be cried. He cried through the yearning for a fix, through more of Edward's words, growing louder and harsher, and through Edward finally pushing him off and slamming the door.

It took a long time for Daniel to stop crying. He felt empty, as if a piece of himself had been gouged out. He tried to fill it with Crystal, tried to sleep it away. But nothing worked. Three weeks later the phone rang.

He was out of his stash, but had no strength to go buy more. His entire body shook with minute tremors. The machine clicked on, and a voice shattered the quiet.

"Daniel, it's Ed. I called your work, but they said you'd been let go." There was a pregnant pause. "Because of the economy." The voice on the other end broke. "I-I hope you're listening to this, Daniel. And not... gone. I've been checking the records at the hospital during my shift, just in case. Nothing yet. I hope I'll never have to see your name there." Another pause. "I'm negative for everything. You should still get tested, just in case." A few seconds of silence followed before the machine clicked off.

Daniel stared across the room at the phone. It was too dangerous to walk to it, though he wanted badly to hear that voice again. Glass littered the floor. His last trip had been bad, the worst.

Days before a nurse from a recovery clinic had called and left her information. He guessed Edward put that request through. House slippers, ones Ed bought for him as a house-warming present, were laying a few feet away. They were thick enough that glass couldn't get through. His eyes flicked to the message machine. To listen to Edward's voice he'd have to listen to the nurse first.

The last time he drank anything or ate must have been yesterday. There was a yawning ache in his stomach that made it hard to walk. Leaning on the table for support, he bumped a pad of paper and pen lying next to the phone. He stared for a moment, between the flashing message number and the blank paper. A week ago he'd broken a vase that Edward found for him in a tiny antique shop along the Oregon coast last year. He'd had some illusion that someone was trying to break in through the window and ended up throwing it at the specter. The pieces still covered the floor, and he sported a nasty cut across his thumb from trying to put it back together. Edward could probably glue it back so that no one could tell it even broke in the first place.

Or maybe they would find another vase. He picked up the pen and pressed it to the paper, waiting as the nurse's voice filtered through. He wrote down the number. Then he sat, listening to Edward's message. When the machine finally clicked off, Daniel had come to a decision. He was going to ask for help this time. He'd lost everything, but there was a chance to get some of it back, and maybe get a second chance to keep those promises he'd made.

COME SPRING
by Matisse Fletcher

He sat alone in the cold wind, a bouquet of fresh flowers lying across his knees. No one else was there, only a few robins looking for worms amongst long grass in need of cutting. They went about their work quietly, casting him beady looks every now and then. But he didn't see them, or much of anything else.

People told him he was handsome for his age, and how much of a looker he must have been in his younger days. His memories now, of summers in denim cut-offs and the blue sky, all smelled of sun.

The cold was bothering his joints, and he knew standing would hurt. Resentment boiled up into his throat, and he grimaced in a tight smile, reaching slowly forward to run his fingers delicately across a name carved into the headstone. The plastic around the flowers crinkled noisily and all the birds darted into the air in a rush of wings and chatter. Behind them they left only the cold wind, gliding over the headstones and statues of angels in one of the city's many graveyards.

"I hope you're not laughing at me somewhere," he said, settling down more comfortably on the wet grass, "for talking to your name. I know you don't believe in anything after, but it's a comfort to me."

Leaning back, he rested on his hands, staring up at the gray sky through the bare branches of a cherry tree. Come Spring the blossoms would bloom soft pink, littering the graves below with thousands of tiny petals.

"You were damn lucky to get this spot. Who knows where they're going to put me." He itched his nose. "Now people are going into holes without coffins, to help the environment." Cutting a glance at the name, he shrugged. "It reminds me of the war too much, what we had to do. What do you think?"

A robin landed on the branch above him, looking down accusingly. Its red chest was a beacon of color against the clouds, the branches like cracks along the marble sky.

"Mariana's fine. Getting old. Like the rest of us." He grinned. "Hope you'll still go for a geezer like me when I come to meet you. To wherever you're listening from, if you are." After a minute, he reached into his pocket and pulled out a picture. "Here it is," he said, waving the picture around. "I found it yesterday when I was cleaning out the attic.

Didn't touch your stuff, I know how you are about that. But you bothered me so much about seeing it." Holding it out gingerly, he pressed it to the icy stone, a shock of sadness nearly splitting him in two. "Wasn't so bad back then, was I? They used to call me quite the ladies man." Laughing, he wiped his eyes. "But I think I would call me more of a gentleman's man." Tucking the picture safely away, he paused to stare at the name. A shaking hand traced the fine letters, one by one. "I was *your* man," he said. Then after a moment, "And don't laugh at me, you old romantic."

He could almost hear the sigh of the wind gently caressing his back and neck. The bouquet was a simple one, of white daisies all neatly arranged among sprigs of baby's breath.

"I've got to get moving. I'm doing a lecture." He sat just a little straighter when he said that. "Down at the Center. About..." Pausing, he looked at the sky again. "HIV, living with it, loving someone with it, and hopefully teaching them why they need to be safe and prevent it." Looking back down at the name, he touched it again, pressing his whole hand flat to the stone, willing warmth into it. "I miss you," he whispered. "And I'm going to tell them that. I don't want them to miss someone like I miss you."

After a few moments the only person in the graveyard that day slowly got up. The daisies were stark white, their little yellow centers vivid among the pale petals. He stood silently for a moment before slowly walking away.

Turning back once, he read the name again, perhaps for the thousandth time. A wash of memories came to him, and he closed his eyes and smelled the sun inside of them.

CHRISTOPHER GASKINS

Born and raised in rural SW Florida, Christopher Gaskins moved to New York City in 1999, looking for the "hustle and bustle" he'd always heard so much about. He currently lives in Brooklyn, where he teaches high school English. In addition to writing poetry, he is an avid reader and record collector. He also volunteers his time at the LGBT Center in Manhattan, handling the finances for one of its major fundraisers, Dance:208. His poems have appeared in such journals as Poet's Paper, The Gay & Lesbian Review, Down in the Dirt, Ganymede and in the anthology Sanctified.

▼

MYSELF
by Christopher Gaskins

I found myself again this evening
hidden
among collected things
and odds and ends in all their places,
tucked away.
    My outgrown self
awaiting sleep
here
along the bottom of all this nighttime, in
the warmth of flannel,
an electric blanket.

HOW OBVIOUS, THEN
by Christopher Gaskins

At 5 a.m., awake and blinking, third day in a row
with a terrible headache,
I am here
in the dark of our dark blue bedroom, our
curtains shut
where morning is evening. From within your arms
and beneath the blanket
I emerge and
stumble
and bump my knee, step around the bed and
out of the door
in search of an aspirin.
It's as I'm returning that you lift your head to ask,
still half in your dream, "You ok?
What's wrong?" Like couples elsewhere,
we've learned
to speak in our own vernacular, to know that this
from you
means how much you love me.

                            How you say
"my boyfriend..."
when teasing my actions or
explaining my habits,
a reference to me as something of yours,
a favorite thing
kept warm in your pocket, familiar
and close; in these boxers
you bought
and then at home requested, "Try them on,"
watching me move
in smiles and longing. It's a kiss
on my shoulder
when you're half-asleep,
the doors

you open and even my hand you caress indirectly.

I come back to bed, slip in
to entangle
against your body and answer, "I have a headache.
I just took some aspirin."
Like couples elsewhere, we all have had
the same conversation. You know
that this from me,
in a disguise of diction, means
"I love you too" –
                    a reworded truth
in these early morning hours.

HINDSIGHT
by Christopher Gaskins

Once, there was this: an ego amazed
at every indulgence of self-satisfaction,
with itself enamored in mutual attraction
and comfort of lies, luxuriously phrased;
all ideas of being – an hyperbole core,
the ego in orbit, surrounding in flight
its "handsomest" day and "know-it-all" night.
Possibly wrong, in error perhaps? The ego ignored
dissention, assistance, any lessening of self.
It believed and it prayed at the altar of youth,
following fun like Narcissus regardless of proof
that resilience ends. Age triumphs in stealth,
experience comes as perfection unravels,
wisdom waits for the ego on the road that it travels.

VIOLET
by Christopher Gaskins

The
fist as a phallus
barreling over itself only to emerge
again, entwine
headfirst

from
out of the unlit hemorrhaging maw
of your anger's
heart, in arc and drop at angled
descent,

fingers
bent-double in making their
stand. I am our
bull's-eye whirlpooling down, all aglow,
come

hither
against my own subconscious, still
yearning you forward
in turn, with each toss of my
beckoning

damage
and plaster-lipped smile, the
bloom, implosion
of masochist's love. The air-
split

arrival,
your hardened intent
hurtling into
and out of my expression's unknown
depths.

TYROBIA HARSHAW

Tyrobia Harshaw is an up and coming author from Seattle, Washington, USA, with poems, short stories, plays, and a novel he is working on. He is grateful to provide readers with a piece of his voice through literature.

▼

FINAL MOMENT OF ILLUMINATION
by Tyrobia Harshaw

The candle wax melted down to the point where the wick wouldn't burn anymore, its cinnamon aroma filled the studio apartment, as promised. The package said it would last for four hours straight. It was running on three hours and thirty-seven minutes when it began to fight for its life, slowly dying out, and the cassette tape remained in the same spot, in the same position Greg left it when he placed it down and lit the match to kill the candle. Within that time, he retrieved a letter and bought a cassette player, tasks which he completed within twenty minutes of lighting the match, so for the other three hours and seventeen minutes, he sat and stared at the tape, slowly mustering up the courage to finally play it.

"Are you just going to stare at it?" he asked himself. He'd been repressing the repetitive thoughts dancing in his head, pushing them into the back of his subconscious, but as the time passed, and the candle slowly whittled away, those two words edged their way into a boding order.

Play it.

"You need to know," he murmured. "It's the only way you'll get closure from the bastard." He nodded in agreement with himself, picked up the tape and the player, paused, then put them both back on the table. "Coward."

He reached into the garbage bin next to him and pulled out a crumpled piece of paper for the third time that day. He neatly flattened it out and reread the words:

> *Dear Greggie,*
> *Hi, baby! I'll just get right down to it. You*
> *asked me to sit in for you during your*
> *father's will reading. I have some bad*
> *news. He didn't leave anything for you.*

"What a surprise," he scoffed.

> *Please don't take it too personally,*
> *sweetheart.*

"Oh I won't. But for argument's sake, just how else should I take it?"

I'm sure he just thought he'd outlive you, and you know how untimely his death was.

"Yea, cancer. *Real* untimely."

He didn't have any time to fix or change it.

"He wouldn't if he did."

He would've if he could've. He loved you. We love you. I hope you know that.

Love,
Mom

P.S.
I know it might not mean much now, but here's something that your father made for you some years ago and never really got around to giving it to you, since you two stopped talking and all. I never listened to it, so I do not know what it says, but hopefully, it will give you some insight on him a little better.

Greg immediately crumpled the letter back up and slam-dunked it in the trash bin. "What was the point of that, huh?" he asked himself. "You're just gonna pull it out of the trash can and read it again, because you're stalling." He slowly began to reach for the tape player. "You're a stronger man than you were when you talked to that son of a bitch. Nothing he can tell you can hurt you. Not anymore." He took the tape and slid it into the player, teasing his fingers around the play button. As he did this, his eyes wandered around the desk and landed on the folded letter that simply had "Greg" written on the front. He set the player to the side and snatched up the paper. "Then why do I still keep *this?*" Silent, angry drips of salt water escaped his tear ducts as he ripped the letter open. It read:

Greg,

Knowing that you, my son, are what you are disgusts me. It literally gets me sick to my stomach. They say that love is unconditional, so I don't understand why you're doing this to your mother and me. What did we do to make you lash out like this? I used to be so proud of you, now I'm not sure I can even look you in the face anymore. I'm writing you this letter because I'm positive if I tell you this in person, I'd end up choking the life out of you. There's only so much you can do before we stop forgiving. It was hard enough when we found out you were a junkie, hooked on that poison, stealing from your own family like we were strangers. Then you got that gay-killer disease and made us believe it was from your needles and the like. Now you tell us that you're...well, I'm done. We're done. You disappoint me, and I say that only because I'm too frustrated to take the time to look up a more appropriate word for it. That might be a word that your mother would use, but I know there's something more fitting in the English language. Saying you're a disgrace is an understatement. You're a waste of my good sperm. I don't want to see or hear from you ever again. Don't consider me your father. Don't consider us family. You're dead to me. Soon, you'll be dead to everyone, as that is God's way of taking care of the problem. What you are isn't natural, and I wish we

could have caught it earlier so we could
have prevented this disease from infecting
you, but the Lord has already bestowed
judgment on your soul with your ailment.
I pray that he has more mercy than I
have for you. I can't forgive you for what
you've done to this family.

John

By the time he'd finished reading, the tears had stopped flowing, and Greg stared blankly at the letter. He'd read that letter so many times, he could probably recite it. He delicately folded the letter back up, set it back down on the table, and picked up the tape recorder. "What, John? You weren't satisfied with the letter? Did you have to tell me how much of a disappointing drugged-out faggot your son turned out to be out loud too?" He pulled the tape out and examined it. It was blank. For all Greg knew, it was empty. "When'd you even do this, anyways?"

*Maybe it's not even **him**,* he thought to himself. *Maybe it's one of those crazy Christian pastor tapes that he always used to order.*

He gave an empty chuckle. "Maybe. Maybe he might've found a tape to *finally* heal the gay in me!"

That'll be the day.

He reached into the garbage bin, pulled out his mother's letter for the fourth time, and dipped it on the candle, into the flame. The flame flung to the side, struggling to keep hold of the last bit of wick before hugging onto the crumpled page, eating away at it, leaving the residue in a black, charred mess. Greg quickly let go and stared into the small burst, mesmerized. "I could do that to it all," he whispered, "then I wouldn't have to worry about it anymore. He's gone from this world, and getting rid of this would make him gone from my life!"

The paper broke off into little bits and hopped in the air, gliding onto his desk. Particles fell onto the player and Greg quickly brushed them off.

Play it.

He picked it up and finally pushed the play button.

"Hey Greg," the recording started, "it's your pop." The voice was crackled and tired, yet stern. "I know the years haven't been too kind to our relationship, but I wanted to get a few things clear to you. Well—

uh—well, son, you know I'm no good talking to you in person, cuz of the arguments and such, so I thought it'd be best to say what I gotta say here on this here tape. No interruptions. No rebuttals. No goddamn mediating from your mother. Just words out of my mouth. For you to hear. From me. True words." The speakers belted out a long sigh.

That's just like you, Greg thought. *You were more of a man than me but not man enough to say this to my face.*

"I know what we've been through is a lot," it continued, "but it's nothing like what you're going to go through now. I told you that if you ever dropped out of high school, I'd disown you, but you dropped out anyway, and we got through that. The drugs—the stealing—I didn't know if we were going to come out of that, but we did. The choices you make in life dictate the consequences that fall upon you, and dropping out got you into drugs, or drugs got you to drop out, I don't know. Drugs got you to the needle. The needle got you stealing for more drugs, and then you got the AIDS.

"You made some piss poor decisions in your life, but you survived from them. And you know what? You're gonna survive the AIDS, too." The playback emoted a couple of sniffles. "You know why I know that? Because you done changed. You got off that stuff. You started getting healthy. You take your meds every day. You've got that sponsor that cares about you so much."

"That was my *lover,*" Greg chuckled.

"You're turning your life around, and I couldn't be more proud than that." The dialogue stopped for a few moments, and the sniffles became gasps and painful moans. "No matter what happens," it continued, slowly, almost in an attempt to keep composure but failing and breaking down completely into sobbing, "you're still my son. I want you to know that no matter what I've said, I'm proud to be your father. I love you son." The playback stopped.

Greg stared down at the tape, indifferent. "I'm not crying," he murmured, voice breaking down. He rewound the tape and replayed it.

As the tape replayed its apology, Greg thought about the letter he read dozens of times, the words that cemented in his brain as his father's overall opinion. The disappointment. The alienation. The insults. The retraction of his birth-given right to have a father. *'Soon, you'll be dead to everyone, as that is God's way of taking care of the problem.'*

"I want you to know that no matter what I've said," the playback continued, "I'm proud to be your fa—"

Greg abruptly stopped the tape. *'Don't consider me your father.'* "Hmph," he grunted, then dropped the tape player on the candle. "I still can't forgive you for what you've done to me." The recorder mashed the remnants of the letter down into ashes, causing it to mix in with the wax as it splashed on the table. The weight of the player was too much for the flame to handle, fluttering around to catch grip. Ultimately, it gave up, exhaling one final time before extinguishing completely.

JACKSON LASSITER

Jackson Lassiter lives and writes in Washington, DC. He is thrilled to be contributing to the Gay City anthology for a second year. His fiction, essays, and poetry have appeared in over 50 journals, anthologies, magazines, and websites. He is currently working on H.A.G.S., a short novel. E-mail him at LuckyJRL@hotmail.com

▼

A FISTFUL OF SERENITY
by Jackson Lassiter

Blood was bound to be shed, that was a given. Only question was – whose? Perhaps the woman behind him in the ticket line – maybe then her yammering would stop.

"Dang, one clerk," she groused. She was tall and thin, pole-like, somewhat unkempt. And she twitched. Nervously. "Doggone, it's only the first day of the Clint Eastwood retrospective. They didn't know there'd be a line?"

But Bobby ignored her. He agreed it was asinine that only one teenaged cashier handled the queue, but he was in no mood to chat. Especially with this canary-in-a-coal-mine. He tuned out her twittering, studied the digital orange letters on the marquee instead. Not that he had to. He had chosen this theater because he needed an Eastwood blood bath, and any one of them would do. He just wanted to watch Clint prove, as he always did, that what's right wasn't always pretty or easy. But it was always necessary.

Fidgeting Woman pressed closer behind him. Her long chin nearly hooked over his right shoulder and her moist breath trickled down the back of his neck.

"This line is barely moving. I'm never going to get a good seat. I hate sitting too close. Or too far away." She spat her worry at him, but her voice softened as she continued, "Clint Eastwood is such a man's man. All the ladies love him. You know he has seven kids? He was sixty-six years old when the last one was born. They have five different mothers. Plus he's been with lots of other women. Barbra Streisand, for one."

Some other day Bobby might not have reacted so harshly to her rapid-fire outpouring of trivia. After all, he agreed with her. Eastwood *was* the man. A real stud. And any guy who had been with Streisand deserved idolatry. But today this woman's anxiety was too real, too palpable, too close. He had to get away from her. Bobby stepped aside, barely out of the ticket line, and turned an insular back. He focused on the movie times with fresh intensity.

"What are you looking at? Did they change the times? Is it sold out?" She moved to his side and studied the marquee with him. She raveled and unraveled a disintegrating white tissue with a quick, jerking motion and then ran her fingers through the slack hair framing her face.

Bobby wished he was here with his mother – catching movies from "the old-days" was one of the special things they shared. She was gracefully enamored of *The Man With No Name*, unlike this blathering Fidgeting Woman. If Mom was here she'd wink at him and whisper, "God grant me the serenity to accept the things I cannot change . . ."

But today he was alone, and instead of hearing his mother's sweet prayer, he heard Fidgeting Woman. Her nasal whine bludgeoned his every nerve.

"Hey! No cuts!"

Without him or Fidgeting Woman noticing, someone had taken *their* spot in line.

"*Go ahead, make my day,*" Bobby said.

* * *

When he visited his mother earlier, he let himself in with the skeleton key he'd had since childhood. His mother used to make him wear it on a string around his neck; she was afraid he would lose it. But now it dangled from his key ring alongside the new-fangled electronic fob that unlocked his waterfront condo, and the thick key to his busy theater costume studio.

The family brownstone usually provided a cool respite from the brutal heat and humidity of the Washington, DC August afternoons, the thick brocade drapes he and his mother stitched years ago on her old Singer machine drawn tight in defense. But today the house had felt worn and stale, and had been permeated with the awful scent that had been there since the cancer took hold of his mother.

"Mom? Hello? Mom!" he had called out. There was no answer. He climbed the stairs and walked the long, dim upper hallway. All the while he feared what he might find. She might be spilled over the stairs in a cascade of death. Or permanently at rest in one of the old wingchairs in the upper landing. Or worse. She could be puddled on the bathroom floor. He would find her heaped on the tiny hexagonal tiles, her thin cotton robe wrenched up over the leaking blue adult diaper in a final act of dehumanization. The ugly end.

But when he looked through the partially open door of her boudoir he saw that she was still flat on her back on the hospital bed. Her wrists intersected over her chest, corpse-like, and her feet, the one part of her that hadn't shriveled, were splayed. Highlighted in bright white orthopedic hose, they dwarfed her deflated body.

Bobby stared across the dim distance of her bedroom, but there was no sign of life. No twitch, no spasm, no movement at all. He turned an ear to better hear, but there was no sound, either. Not a snore, a wheeze, or a rattle. Nothing.

He moved to her bedside, holding his breath against that sickening odor, and looked down at her, at the dry flakes of her scalp beneath the thin fuzz of white hair and the way her lower jaw hung open. *If she's passed,* he thought, *I should close her mouth before rigor mortis locks it open. She would hate anyone seeing her like this.*

Bobby trembled as he lifted one hand from the crossbones over her heart. His third grade teacher had used a pair of caged rabbits to teach the class the miracle of reproduction, perhaps to sway back to the heterosexual fold those she suspected were already moving away from that calling. His mother's hand felt very much like the wriggling pink newborn Miss Knapp had pressed hopefully into his small palm. Hairless skin sliding over the lumps and bulges of delicate bones. A clawing rodent infant, his mother's gnarled claw. Panic.

Then her fingers fluttered in his and she awoke. They both exhaled as her rheumy eyes focused. "Bobby," she whispered.

He moved her dead weight to the bedside wheelchair and gave her two of the Oxycodone that no longer kept her pain at bay. Then he retreated toward the kitchen to heat some soup for her lunch, detouring to the back porch for fresh air and a cigarette. The nicotine settled his nerves. A lawnmower buzzed in the distance and the sound of boys at play dribbled over the fences separating the back lots along the alley. Bobby remembered his own solitary childhood, the hours spent in the sewing room with his mother, the other boys' taunts as he hurried home from school.

"Hey, *Roberta,* going in to help your mama sew now?"
He had kept current with these boys' lives through the years. Even after moving across town, he came home every day for lunch. His mother fed him the neighborhood news along with whatever she had cooked. Vincent was sent to jail, she told him over meatloaf. Tax fraud. Edward lost his job and their family's home. Tyrone was in rehab. Again.

Bobby butted the cigarette in the powdery dirt beneath some potted marigolds gone dead from neglect. It was time to heat the soup.

These days she barely woke when he brought her the lunch he fixed. She just sat with her chin resting on the bones of her chest, her involuntarily gaping mouth forced shut by the weight of her head. But today, when Bobby hooked the tray over the arms of the wheelchair, she stirred and shifted in the green plastic seat. She lifted the spoon and then, as she did before every meal, she recited her favorite prayer. "God grant me the serenity to accept the things I cannot change, the courage to change the things I can, and the wisdom to know the difference."

The words elicited a familiar memory, but this time it spilled across him hard like an avalanche. The vignette was unremarkable, but he remembered every detail. Twilight sliced horizontally across the room. She was a young woman; Bobby was still a toddler. She leaned over the white enameled side rail of his crib and recited the prayer in a sing-song voice. Her dark hair was pleated into a thick braid that tumbled over one shoulder. She smelled like Lux soap, and the wallpaper behind her was – still was today – pale ivory and festooned with clumps of dark purple plums and bright green, teardrop-shaped leaves. When she left the nursery, a wicker laundry basket perched on one hip, she paused in the doorway and smiled back at him. And then he was alone with the fruits and her words. First memory.

Twenty-seven words he had heard for forty-seven years. Diaper rash, father's burial, puberty's angst, his sexuality – all scabs his mother soothed with the salve of this prayer. Over time the words inserted themselves in his reflexes. At first blush of pain or bruise of ego, his mother's calm voice came to him: accept or change, but do so wisely.

Today, though, she barely eked out the words, more a plea than a prayer, and then without swallowing even one bite of soup she dropped the spoon and asked to be put back to bed.

"Bobby, this is no way to live," she mumbled before closing her eyes.

"It's going to be OK," he answered as he smoothed her fly-away hair, "I promised." But she didn't hear him. Her mouth fell open as she drifted off.

* * *

The scent of greasy popcorn curled Bobby's stomach as Line Cutter gave him and Fidgeting Woman the evil eye. "You two better not fuck with me. I didn't cut; you were looking at the marquee. I just got in line while you were making up your minds."

Fidgeting Woman huffed. "I was in line. I already know what I am seeing. *A Fistful of Dollars.* You cut."

Bobby just laughed. "Look," he said, pointing to Fidgeting Woman. "*The Good . . .*" He pointed to himself. "*The Bad . . .*" and then he pointed to Line Cutter. "*And the Ugly.*"

Just then the line moved forward and, like a steam engine crossing the vast landscape in one of the old spaghetti westerns, they all chugged closer to Clint. Bobby and the woman moved back into line but the squatter held fast and hobbled forward with them. When they stalled again, he and Bobby stood face-to-face. From beneath the mop of his tousled black hair, Line Cutter's needle-sharp eyes stabbed at Bobby.

"You looking for a fight, faggot?" Line Cutter punctuated his question with a sharp poke to the chest, a one-fingered shove that caught Bobby off guard. He stumbled backwards.

* * *

Bobby's mother always arched her brows during the second line of the supplication. They angled up toward God, stretched up like hands rising in a hallelujah chorus. Those eyebrows had faith in the message. ". . . the courage to change the things I can," she would say, forehead clasped in prayer.

After pouring the soup down the disposal and rinsing the dishes, Bobby had wandered the quiet house. Every nook held a secret; every window jamb and cabinet pull prompted a memory. Here was where his mother found his father laid out after the heart attack. Everyone had always said it would be the drink that got him, but he fooled them.

That credenza held his mother's purse, middle drawer on the right. Bobby had pilfered smokes from it, hiding and choking in the garage until it felt natural. In later years he and his mother would share cigarettes like they shared their best-friend secrets.

And that is the table at which his mother served the soup *she* warmed for *him.*

Everything in the brownstone was familiar yet unfamiliar, all of it an askew rendition of what used to be. The rooms seemed smaller than they once were, and as Bobby paced their limits the walls heaved further inward. And that horrid, acidic scent persevered. He repeated his mother's prayer over and over.

At the foot of the stairs, a loose floorboard squeaked beneath the outdated orange and yellow carpet. It used to be he knew every loose board, every noise the old floor made. In his teens, he crept through the nighttime shadows of this house, slunk out undetected to meet like-minded boys and returned, hours later, beneath his mother's loving radar. But there was no longer reason to sneak. Even if she hadn't years ago embraced the life her only son lived, what remained upstairs was no longer her.

Bobby rocked back and forth on the disjointed plank, his left hand caressing the smooth round finial at the banister's end. The floorboard protested with a steady rhythm – squeak-squeak, squeak-squeak, squeak-squeak – like a persistent, nagging heartbeat. He slowed his movement until the sound ceased. Dead silence.

Bobby made his way back to his mother's side. There, he hovered.

Her chest lifted and fell in a shallow but regular pattern, her heart and lungs refusing to stop even though the rest of her body had given up. Again her mouth dangled open. The toothless pink cavern glistened in the dim light.

Bobby lifted the spare pillow, fluffed its feathers, and then pressed it to her face. He pushed hard, a hand on each side of the head to seal the mouth and nose. The body convulsed once, twice, and then the right arm weakly flailed. It made one reflexive, aimless punch that connected with nothing, and then settled gently back to the bed. All was still. Bobby kept pressing on the pillow, and between his sobs he counted aloud in a slow-paced rhythm: "One, two, three . . .," all the way to twenty. He had to make certain the deed was done; there was no turning back. When he finally removed the pillow she didn't move. He wiped his eyes and felt for a pulse on her wrist and then her neck. Nothing.

Bobby closed his mother's mouth but it fell open again, so he lifted the surprising heft of her head and wadded the guilty pillow beneath it. Her face tipped forward; her mouth latched shut. And that is how he left her for Miss Agnes, the visiting nurse, to find.

* * *

Line Cutter swung wide. His powerful arm ended in a tight fist that connected with the left side of Bobby's head, knocking him to the garish carpet. Fidgeting Woman scurried to the cashier without a backwards glance as Line Cutter hurled himself at Bobby, throwing wild punches that crunched into his face. But Bobby felt no pain. He felt only the blood pouring from his nose. It was warm, red absolution. Then two policemen yanked the slugger off him and it was over.

He mouthed *thank you* to Line Cutter as he was dragged away.

Bobby retreated to the men's room to wash. Calmed, bleeding stopped, he returned to the now-empty queue. He paid for a ticket and begged a cup of ice, and then made his way toward the dark, safe embrace of the theater. The previews had begun, and in the faint blue light of the projector Bobby saw Fidgeting Woman squirming in her seat. He moved as far away as possible, where he held the ice to the swelling tenderness of his face and waited for the movie to begin.

"And the wisdom to know the difference," Bobby said to no one in particular.

URSULA K. LE GUIN

Ursula K. Le Guin lives in Portland, Oregon. Among her honors are a National Book Award, five Hugo and five Nebula Awards,18 Locus Awards, the Kafka Award, a Pushcart Prize, and the Harold D. Vursell Memorial Award from the American Academy of Arts and Letters. She received the Library of Congress Living Legends award in the "Writers and Artists" category in April 2000. In 2004, Le Guin was received the Association for Library Service to Children's May Hill Arbuthnot Honor Lecture Award and the Margaret Edwards Award.

▼

IN THE DROUGHT
by Ursula K. Le Guin

For Judith and Ruth

Sarah was watering the tomato plants, letting the water flow from the hose along the tunnel between the big droopy messy bushes promiscuously mingling their green and red and yellow and little pearshaped and middlesized plumshaped and big tomatoshaped tomatoes so that she couldn't tell which one grew on which of the six plants. She ate a little yellow pearshaped one. It was like tart honey in her mouth. The marvelous bitter smell of the leaves was on her hands now. She thought it was time to get a basket and pick some of the reddest and yellowest ones, but only after she finished watering; there were still the two old roses needing a drink, and the youngest azalea looked very thirsty. Late afternoon light struck through the air at a long angle, making the water from the hose seem reddish. She looked again; there must be rust coming through the pipes. The flow from the end of the hose was reddish-brown, and increasingly opaque. She held up the hose and let the stream arch out so she could watch it. The color deepened fast to crimson. Striking the earth it made puddles of that intense and somber color on the dirt, slow to soak in. She had not touched the faucet, but the flow had increased. The red stream shooting from the end of the hose looked thick, almost solid. She did not want to touch it.

She set the hose down in the runnel and went to the stand- pipe to turn it off. It seemed wrong to water plants with water that looked like that. Puzzled and uneasy, she went up the two I back stairs and into the kitchen, hooking the screen door shut behind her with a practised foot. Belle was standing at the sink. "There's something funny," Sarah began, but Belle looked at her and said, "Look"

From the arched steel faucet ran a red stream, spattering on the white enamel of the sink and pooling in the strainer before it ran down the drain.

"It must be the hotwater heater," Belle said.

"The garden hose is doing it too," Sarah said.

After a while Belle said, "It must be the drought. Something in the reservoirs. Mud from the bottom of the lakes, or something."

"Turn it off," Sarah said.

Belle turned off the hot tap. Then slowly, as if compelled, she turned on the cold tap. The red, thick flow spurted out, spattering heavily. Belle put her finger into the stream. "Don't!" Sarah said,

"It's hot," Belle said. "Almost hot." She turned it off.

They watched the red drops and splatters slide sluggishly towards the drain.

"Should we call the plumber?" Belle said, "No, I guess not— but the city water thing, water department, bureau? Do you think? But I suppose it's happening to everybody, everybody would be calling at once, wouldn't they. Like earthquakes."

Sarah went into the front room and looked out the picture window, over the brown grass and across the street. The lawn sprinkler on the Mortensons' lawn was still going. Sunday evening was one of the two days a week watering was permitted under the drought restrictions. You were supposed to water only by hand and only shrubs and vegetable gardens, but Mr. Mortenson turned on his little lawn sprinkler and nobody said anything or reported him. He was a big man with two big teen-age sons who rode motorbikes. He never spoke to Belle and Sarah and never looked at them. The sons never spoke, but sometimes they looked, staring while they talked with their friends who came in pickups and on motorbikes. Mr. Mortenson was in his carport cutting firewood, the whine of the power saw rising to a scream, stopping abruptly, starting again. Mrs. Mortenson had gone by an hour ago on her way to church; she went morning and evening on Sundays. She always looked away from Belle and Sarah's house when she passed it.

The telephone rang, and Sarah answered it to shut it up. It was Neenie. "Sarah! The darndest thing! You won't believe! I went to pee and I looked in the toilet, you know, I just noticed, and it was all red and I thought, oh, my heavens, I've got my period, and then I thought, but I'm sixty-six! And I had a hysterectomy, didn't I? And so I thought, oh, oh no, it's my kidneys, I going to die, but I went to wash my hands, and the water came out of the faucets all red. So it isn't me, it has to be the city water, isn't that the strangest thing? Maybe some kind of fraternity joke thing? Eleanor thinks it's mud, because the water up in the watershed is so low, from the drought, but I called the city and they said nobody had reported any abnormalities. I don't suppose your water's coming funny, is it?"

"Yes," Sarah said, standing watching the low sunlight strike through the crystal showers from Mr. Mortenson's sprinkler. "Listen,

Neenie, I'll call you back, I have to make a call now. Don't worry about it. OK?"

"No, no, I won't worry, it just seems so strange, goodbye," Neenie said hurriedly. "Love to Belle!"

Sarah called Andrew and got his recorded voice: "Hullo! Sorry, Tom and I aren't doing the telephone just now; but we'll get back to you soon." She waited for the beep and said, "Andrew, this is Sarah," and paused, and said, "Is there something funny with—" and Andrew came on the line: "Hub, Sarah! I was monitoring? Tom says I mustn't feel guilty about monitoring."

"Andrew, this is weird, but is your water OK? Your tap water?'

"Should I look?"

"Yes, would you?"

While Sarah waited, Belie came into the room. She straightened the afghan on the sofa and stood looking out across the street.

"Their water looks all right," she said.

Sarah nodded.

"Rainbows," Belle said.

Andrew came back on the line after a considerable time. "Hello, Sarah. Did you taste it?"

"No," she said, seeing again the thick, strong, bright-red rush of it from the hose.

"I did," he said, and paused. "I asked Mrs. Simpson in the apartment downstairs. They have water. Not—what we have."

"What should we do?" Sarah said.

"Call the city," he said vigorously. "We pay for our water. They can't let this happen!"

"Let it happen?"

After a little while Andrew said, "Well, then, we can't let it happen."

"I'll call around," Sarah said.

"Do that. I'll call Sandy at the paper. We can't just...."

"No," she said. "We can't. Call me back if you find out anything. Or decide anything."

"You too. OK? Talk to you soon. Chin up, not the end of the world!" He hung up; Sarah hung up and turned to Belle. "We'll get something going," she said. "There's a good network."

Belle went back to the kitchen, and Sarah followed her. Belle turned both taps full on. The red rush from the faucet spattered and coiled on the enamel. "Don't, don't," Sarah whispered, but Belle put her hands in the stream, turning and rubbing them together, washing them. "There are songs about this," she said. "But they're not my songs." She turned off the taps and deliberately wiped her hands on the white-and-yellow dishtowel, leaving great smears and clots that would soon stiffen and turn brown. "is don't like city water," she said. "Never did. Or small town water. It tastes funny. Tastes like sweat. Up in the mountains, you could drink from little creeks that run right out of the glaciers, out of the snowmelt. Like drinking air. Drinking sky Bubbles without the champagne. I want to go back up to the mountains, Sarah."

"We'll go," Sarah said. "We'll go soon." They held each other for a while, close, silent. "What are we going to drink?" Sarah whispered. Her voice shook.

Belle loosened her hold and leaned back a bit; she stroked Sarah's hair back from her face. "Milk," she said. "We'll drink milk, love."

STEVE MACISAAC

Too contemplative to be porno and too explicit to be anything else, the three issues released to date of Steve MacIsaac's SHIRTLIFTER all examine the intersection of sexuality, personality, and society. STICKY, his collaboration with Dale Lazarov, was released by Bruno Gmünder in 2006. Current work in progress can be seen three days a week at ModernTales.com, or at his website, stevemacisaac.com

▼

You Do the Math

by Steve MacIsaac

89

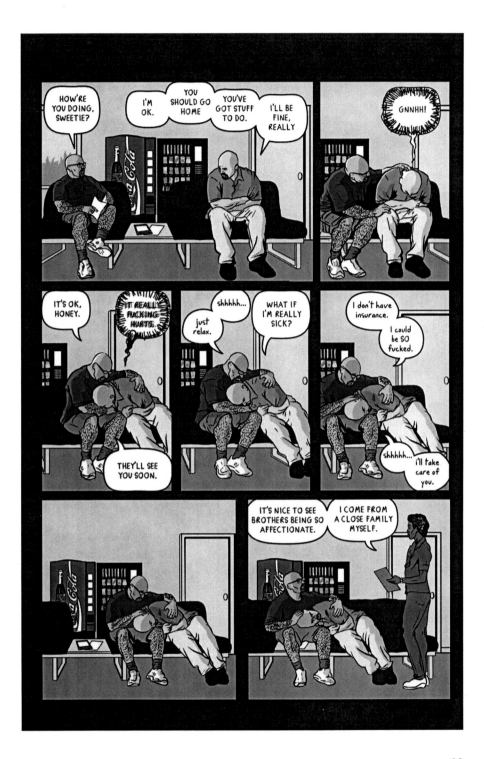

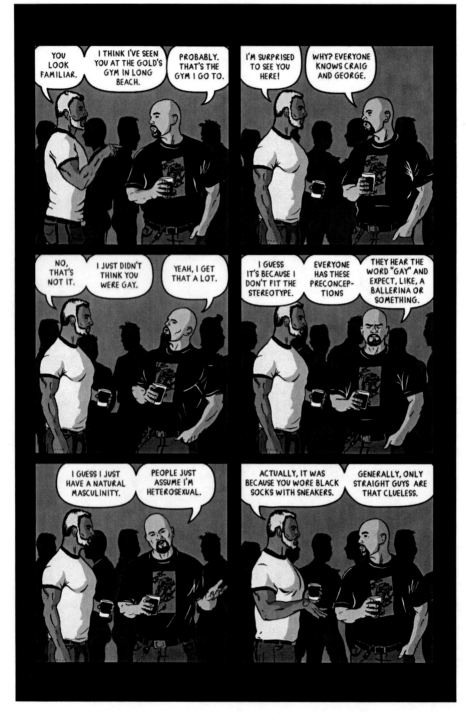

CRAIG MARTIN

Soon after he moved to Seattle, Craig's poetry appeared in the Northwest Gay & Lesbian Reader. In retrospect he recalls that his writing grew less angry when he came out. He recently exhibited a series of photos taken at Seattle's Green Lake, and has begun writing a novel, Hard \ Air. See more at www.craigtmartin.com

▼

BROADWAY
by Craig Martin

I like Broadway—the one in Seattle—though some of my friends think it's too Gay. What I like is the sense of community. It seems easier to feel at home among 50,000 (or however many we are) Gay people, than among Seattle's half million.

When I was coming out in the '70's, I became aware of this street as a sort of geographic locus of Gay Seattle sensibilities. It seemed possible/likely that anyone here might be Gay—waiters at the Dilettante, browsers at Bailey/Coy Books, diners at the Deluxe.

At first, newly/barely out, I was self-conscious—paranoid—that, for example, someone might see me buying the Seattle Gay News. Walking Broadway, quarter ready in my sweaty fingers, I walked past news vending machines until I felt no one was looking, then thrust my quarter in and quickly folded the SGN under my arm.

Later I grew to feel at home walking here and as a regular at stores and restaurants. Some days, looking for something to do, I'd drive across town to Broadway to see what was happening.

Like today, walking down Broadway. Today, poised on the curb at Thomas, waiting for the walk light, but thinking about last weekend.

A different place entirely: driving back over Stevens Pass, the weather splendid, the mountain scenery extraordinary. One particular slope seemed special. Rugged rock outcroppings jutting through fir and hemlock as they thinned upslope to the final outcrop of bare summit mass. Conifer greens matching rock grays against the crystal sky, and my heart wanting to be up in that place.

There, above the road, was profoundly "explorable territory." I wished it were earlier in the day, and I, not in such a rush, could park and explore all afternoon.

Although I drove on to Seattle: In my mind I found a stream that tumbled through talus-strewn slopes. Leaves, caught in sunlight, fluttered to the water surface. At a tiny waterfall I turned up from the stream, to the base of a white rock cliff. Living rock, hard and cool to touch. Clambering over boulders, I followed the base of the cliff until I could climb up alongside it and step out on its grassy lip. I lay back then and hungrily breathed crisp air. My fingers felt unseen the mix of soft grass and jagged gravel. Shards pricked through, energizing my skin. Above, a hawk or vulture circled silently, and I closed my eyes, enjoying the red warmth of sun through eyelids.

The light at Broadway and Thomas turns to "walk." As I step off the curb, so does a young man on the opposite side of the street. I see his shining eyes; his T-shirt fluttering in the breeze, loose fitting, not tucked into his Levis. I see his Levis and realize I am thinking: there also is profoundly explorable territory.

STEPHEN MEAD

In the 1990s Stephen Mead's poems began appearing in literary journals, but after moving to Massachusetts, Stephen concentrated on painting. In 2000 Stephen started seeking publication again for his writing and art combined. Since then his work has appeared internationally. In 2004 Stephen began experimenting with poetry/art hybrids, creating award-winning e-books such as "Heroines Unlikely". From there Stephen began experimenting with his art/poems as films. In 2006 Stephen released a CD of poems set to music, "Safe & Other Love Poems", (CDBaby.com), as well as three DVDs, (Indieflix.com). In 2007, print editions of his work began being distributed by Amazon.com and Blurb.com.

▼

SAFE KISS 1
by Stephen Mead

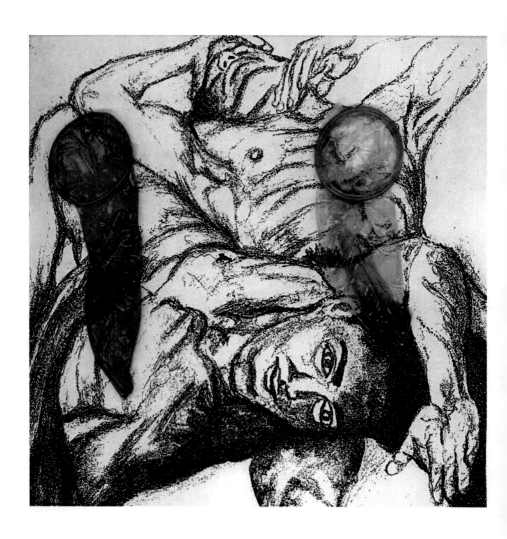

SAFE KISS 4
by Stephen Mead

Russ Morgan

I'm a gay man who makes chandeliers from upcycled materials (www.justarumor.com) who discovered a passion for taking erotically charged photographs of men. I like simple, relaxed poses with natural light that celebrate the beauty of men. I feel it's important to make a connection with the models, allowing them to feel at ease, thus getting their personalities reflected in their photographs. "Capture your beauty while it's still obvious!" See more of my photographs at www.RussMorganPhotography.com.

▼

ERIC ORNER

Eric Orner is a cartoonist and animation storyboard artist whose comics and graphic stories have appeared in Newsweek, The New Republic and The San Francisco Chronicle. In 2006 a feature film based on Eric's widely published comic strip, "The Mostly Unfabulous Social Life of Ethan Green" was released nationally in cinemas across the USA. The comic strip has been anthologized in 4 books from St. Martin's Press. For ten years after college and law school Eric also worked as a counsel on the staff of Congressman Barney Frank.

▼

ALONE IN ABU TOR- A YEAR IN JERUSALEM
by Eric Orner

ISRAELIS DON'T LIKE YOU TO BE ALONE: "EAT ALONE, DIE ALONE", MY COWORKER NOAM IS ALWAYS TELLING ME AT LUNCH WHEN I'M JONESING FOR A SANDWICH IN FRONT OF MY COMPUTER.

APPARENTLY AYELET, THE COMPANY CEO, WHO HAS NEVER BEFORE BOTHERED WITH ME FOR SO MUCH AS A BOCHER TOV, IS SUDDENLY CONCERNED FOR MY WELFARE. SHE'S ON THE PHONE NOW WITH MICHAL, OUR CRAFTY DEPARTMENT SECRETARY.

MICHAL COMES UP WITH A BRILLIANT, ON-THE-SPOT LIE...

"YOU OWE ME, ORNERICO", SHE SAYS,
FLIPPING HER CELL SHUT.

I DECIDE TO TAKE THE BOTTLES TO THE RECYCLING.
ANOTHER THING ABOUT THIS PLACE IS, ITS GOT THIS CONTRARY THING IT
DOES WHERE, IF YOU WALK SOMEWHERE, AND THE WHOLE WAY IS UPHILL...

IT'S NICE TO GET SOME AIR THOUGH, AND I'M TAKING IN THE OTHERWORDLY
VIEWS FROM OUTSIDE MY PLACE...

LATER, MY BIG PLANS FOR THE LONG HOLIDAY WEEKEND ARE EBBING AWAY.
THE STILLNESS OF SHABBAT IN JERUSALEM DOES THAT TO YOU. ONE MINUTE
IT'S 9AM ON A FRIDAY MORNING AND YOU'RE ALL SET TO TAKE THE RENTED
CAR WAY UP NORTH TO THE GAY BEACH AT GA'ASH. THE NEXT, IT'S NOON
AND YOU'RE THINKING MAYBE YOU'LL NAP A LITTLE LONGER.

ITS 2PM. ITS HOT. THE GUY UPSTAIRS YOU'VE NEVER SEEN IS SINGING AND
STRUMMING HIS GUITAR. HE DRIFTS DOWN TO YOU FROM THE BALCONIES
IN BACK...

AT 3 PM THERE'S A DISTURBANCE IN THE FRENCH GIRL'S ROOM. LIKE ME SHE'S A FOREIGN NATIONAL WORKING AT THE COMPANY, BUT I RARELY SEE HER IN THE BIG APARTMENT WE SHARE. MOSTLY SHE'S IN HER ROOM HAVING SEX WITH HER ISRAELI BOYFRIEND.

NOW THOUGH, SHE'S SCREAMING.

THERE MUST BE ANOTHER SPIDER...
JERUSALEM HAS BIG SPIDERS...

REALLY BIG.

LIKE SMART CARS WITH FUR, BIG.

I DECIDE TO TAKE THE BOTTLES TO THE RECYCLING.
ANOTHER THING ABOUT THIS PLACE IS, IT'S GOT THIS CONTRARY THING IT
DOES WHERE, IF YOU WALK SOMEWHERE, AND THE WHOLE WAY IS UPHILL . .

EXTRAVAGANTLY REUNITED, WE MAKE OUR EXCUSES TO MOSHE
AND BLOW THIS SCHWARMA STAND...

IT'S 4 PM ON A SHABBAT AFTERNOON. A MUEZZIN IS SOUNDING
OFF FROM LOUDSPEAKERS ATOP A MINARET NEARBY. THE CAT AND
I SNACK ON SOME OLIVES AND DOZE. NEITHER OF US NEEDS TO
BE ANYWHERE TILL MONDAY.

IN THE QUIET STILLNESS OF THE HOLIDAY I'VE FORGOTTEN TO BE VIGILANT ABOUT MOSHE WHO WANTS ME TO READ A SCREENPLAY HE'S WRITTEN ABOUT HIS RIGHT-WING, PRO-SETTLER SELF...

POLITICS ASIDE THOUGH, AND NOT TO BE A TOTAL MISANTHROPIC JERK, BUT MOSHE IS COMA-INDUCING TO EXCHANGE SHALOMS WITH... READING AN ENTIRE SCREENPLAY OF HIS HAS GOTTA BE LETHAL IS WHAT I'M THINKING, TOTALLY MISANTHROPICALLY JERKILY, WHEN, LUCKILY...

...ZE'EVI, THE STRAY CAT WHO'S ADOPTED ME, IS ALL OF A SUDDEN BRUSHING UP AGAINST MY LEG...

..."OMIGOSH!" I TRILL, "SWEETHEART! YOU'VE COME BACK!"

IN FACT, ZE'EVI HASN'T BEEN ANYWHERE. I FED HER 20 MINUTES BEFORE TAKING THE BOTTLES. UNLIKE JERUSALEM DOGS HOWEVER, JERU'S CATS ARE UP FOR THIS SORT OF DUPLICITY, AND ZEEVI, FOR MOSHE'S BENEFIT, YOWLS THEATRICALLY, AS IF SHE'S SPENT THE PAST THREE WEEKS

EXTRAVAGANTLY REUNITED, WE MAKE OUR EXCUSES TO MOSHE AND BLOW THIS SCHWARMA STAND...

ITS 4 PM ON A SHABBAT AFTERNOON. A MUEZZIN IS SOUNDING OFF FROM LOUDSPEAKERS ATOP A MINARET NEARBY. THE CAT AND I SNACK ON SOME OLIVES AND DOZE. NEITHER OF US NEEDS TO BE ANYWHERE TILL MONDAY.

A TYLER PERRY

Tyler focuses his work on the personal-as-political, continually inspired by the works of Lorca, Whitman, Difranco, and Hardy. He's trained with Bent Writing Institute, bound his poesía en Español, and attempted, in often improvised ways, to queer syntax and grammar as interventions in everyday life.

▼

TAXATION: A PROSTITUTE'S DREAM
by A Tyler Perry

For 2008, I deduct:
30 bottles of magnum steel lube,
20 sets of linens,
57,000 dollars in business dinners,
5 Prada loafers, 3 Ferragamos, and 2 Dolce&Gabanas,
30,000 in wardrobe and accessories,
50 plane tickets,
3 cell phones,
and 24,000 dollars for the downtown flat.

all in all, 2008 could be a good year,
for Uncle Sam and hopefully me.

but how could you too declare
such a lascivious litany of deductions?
it's easy: just legalize prostitution.

it's about time
we open our capitalistic arms and legs
and get back to the basics.
forget priesthood, counseling, medicine, or education.
those helping professions
seem to only help those with access
to the right front doors.

the unrecognized profession of fucking,
sucking, and ducking down below
the radar of america
seems to be the most promised land
and best service to our community
that literally does any body good.

and what of this should scare anyone?

what scares me is that
we've got STD's on the rise,
men who leave their wives every morning
for the "gym" to work out on the thigh master
of their gay boy-toy,
licensed masseurs giving more
than their business card after a naturopathic rub down,
slews of slutty ads as the revenue back bones

of our mainstream radical press,
gaggles of young girls
bearing it all on the lunch breaks
of slobbery tongued business men,
blue collar masses putting out
in-human energy, time, and taxes
to buttress the backs of white collar classes,
republican-fed world health agendas
of abstinence and celibacy
instead of legitimizing the most common agenda of
the human race: sex,
fuck, we've got our fellow human beings going without
instead of feeling safe to put out.

yet, we abstain in doing anything above-the-belt
about this crisis below all our belts.
we stew in chastity, masking libidinal passions,
longing for a morsel of after-glow in our 9 to 5 lives.
Uncle Sam still refuses to publicly announce
that one of the best driving forces
to our free market economy
is the tall economic indicator in your pants.

alas, our legions of sex workers are
degraded, declassified, and black-listed,
we leave them to destitute streets,
back alley boogies, unsheathed cocks,
debilitating viruses, coat-hanger procedures,
and the cold metal handcuffs of
perverted peeping police officers.

imagine a free world for sex workers
and I will show you
better business districts
less red light ghettos,
increased access to healthcare
a decreased need for it,
lower levels of public health crises
better manicured pubic hair styles,
less hard-up's, more hard-on's,
better self-perception, less physique obsession,
heads held higher, more bobbing lower,
bigger smiles from passer-bys
and wetter dreams for water-cooler klatches.

and, maybe, just maybe
there'd be a new convert,
card-carrying member
trying to live out every orgiastic,
Internal Revenue Service-evading fantasy.
little naked me.

(PERRY, 2008)
by A Tyler Perry

I have a confession to make.
I mean, maybe it's more of a disclosure,
a coming-clean even.
I just I have to admit that I have an intellectual fetish:
I like parentheses.

actually, I love to think about what's in parentheses.
inside them, in between them, nestled in the middle,
cogitating on what's being referenced.
eg, for example
ie, that is
aka, also known as
cf, as compared to
or, even better, *who's* being referenced,
like in this moment: (Perry, 2008).

citation chains.
those are the real meat of what gets me going
after all these habituating years of academic life.

"the 'essential enemy' is the status quo of the
bourgeoisie."
(Roland Barthes, 1970)

I've come to realize that our living depends on our
citations.
whether they're a function of social capital,
privileged positionality, eclectic intersectionality,
poised pedigree, or desirable geography
it seems to me that the sexiest piece of it all
is to ponder what that little name and date are *doing*
what they *allow for* the speaker to do
what they *will for* in the world they create
right there on the page, in black-and-white,
and, more importantly, out there in the real world

when our citations are animated by people and politics.

"every tool is a weapon, if you hold it right."
(Ani Difranco, 1996)

in between material or proverbial double parentheses,
a citation manifests so succinctly
the person, the thing, the instance before us
upon which we're building
connoting a trail,
a pathway that we're on, that we buy into
mythologizing for ourselves and others
who we are, what we do, where we've been
and unconsciously or not,
how we oblige our readers
to think about themselves, their behavior, their thoughts
as natural and normal in everyday life.

"the real problem under the banner of Nation today is
hetero-normativity."
(Michael Warner, 2002)

used prudently, citations *do not* confine
the parameters of our thoughts and speech
instead they open up the possibilities
to where we're going.
they prove to others that we're erecting
on top of something else,
standing on someone else.
and even though our words are bounded end-by-end
by those little arched lines,
our citations legitimize when we step *out of* bounds.
they can link us from one moment in time
to a world yet-in-the-making,
a world beyond what exists now
to one that we would hope to walk in some day
if we had the power to set the terms.

"who cannot not want rights?"
(Gayatri Spivak, 1996)

who cannot not want the veneer, the imagined comfort,
the fragile promise from institutions
and frontline civil servants
that you will (someday) be treated "equal" and "fair"
before The Law,
that you will (someday) be cited in public record.
our incessant investment to be part of
the machine of nation systems
cannot be disentangled from
the ways people are disenfranchised differentially
by those exact same systems and civilians,
cannot be separated from how certain existences
are left out of the middle of our privileging parentheses,
cannot be divorced from the ironic pleas that
"we're just like you."

"one of the real accomplishments of neoliberalism
today
is it has provided for certain gay people an ethos of
homo-normativity, or a rainbow replication of
heteronormativity, accepting new forms of inequality *in
exchange for* juridical and market rights."
(Lisa Duggan, 2004)

recently, a gaggle of upstanding white gay men
were walking in what-they-thought-to-be
their gay borough of our local democratic district.
these men tried to *verbally* take on taunters and teasers,
but were *physically* over taken
by homophobic force and fists.
consequently, I inquired publicly
to a darling of our local democratic party
how exactly new domestic partnership laws
and wallet cards
would address the real world threats to safety
that queer people face
yesterday, today, and tomorrow
alongside our newly minted citations
and privileges in public law.

the response?: "gay people just need to grow up."
(Jason Paulson, 2007)

citation-by-citation,
the guts of our faggotry constituency
are increasingly side-lined by a singularly-defined
political positionality
cited to the masses as the logical consequence
of a national queer conquest,
and sold to the gay classes as a precursor
to a larger piece-meal project
that has got all our backs,
just long enough to step on all of them,
all in the name of development! progress!
our march in time forward!

it's as if the whole-sale purchase of holy matrimony
comes at the expense of the people
who are cited to be protected,
including those of us intellectual fairies
who have the proclivity to ask questions,
those of us who may have the predilection
to reference a different circumstance,
or those of us who may simply and consciously
make a different citation
for what social justice is
and how we might get there together
without leaving anyone behind.

"another world is not only possible, She is on Her way.
on a quiet day, I can hear Her breathing."
(Arundhati Roy, 2003)

JACKSON PHOTOGRAFIX

Jackson is a Canadian self-taught photographer. After spending over a decade in NYC shooting the male form, he continues to explore new territory in creating underivative homoerotic imagery. His work has been seen throughout North America in exhibition and in publication, both print and online. He has been included in two volumes of The World's Greatest Erotic Art of Today, and his website (jacksonphotografix.com) was selected as one of the world's best in quality and content in the 2005 book Erotic Websites. For the past two years he has shown his photography with the ARTundressed Tour and the Exposure Festival in Edmonton, Alberta, Canada. Jackson loves Seattle and has been delighted to also present his work annually at the Seattle Erotic Arts Festival.

Jackson's work also appears on the cover of this volume.

▼

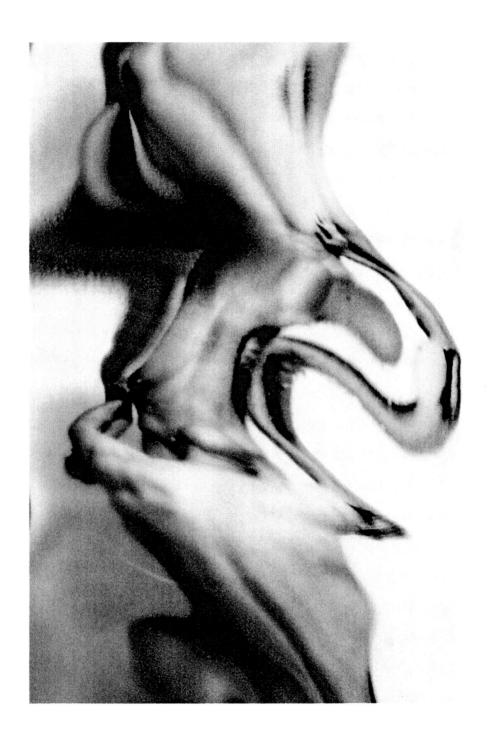

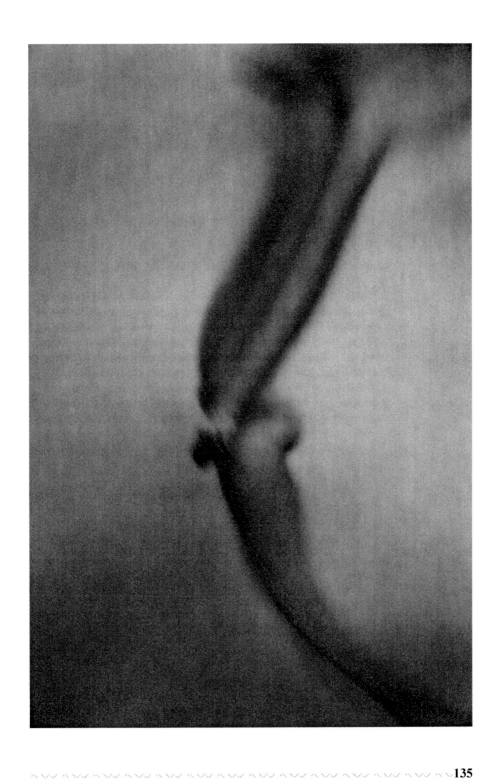

MARTIN POUSSON

Martin Pousson was born and raised in Acadiana, in the bayouland of Louisiana. His first novel, No Place, Louisiana, was published by Riverhead Books and was a finalist for the John Gardner Award in fiction. His first collection of poetry, Sugar, was published by Suspect Thoughts Press and was a finalist for the Lambda Literary Award. His stories and poems have appeared in Epoch, Icon, Parnassus, Transfer, The Louisiana Review, The New Delta Review, New Orleans Review and Cimarron Review. He currently teaches at California State University, Northridge and is at work on a collection of stories, The Nerves.

▼

REVOLVER
by Martin Pousson

Leave it to my uncle to clear up the whole
mess. AIDS is not a plague, but a blessing

from God. It's the homo himself who's
the pariah, the problem.

A mortal sin, he calls it, same as murder.
AIDS is not a plague, but a revolver.

Son, he says, you're shooting fair game.
You're shooting yourself.

Decalogue ('85-'95)
by Martin Pousson

I.

The test had been handled by a plasma donor center, where I went under the needle twice a week in exchange for extra cash for all the booze and tabs of acid that fueled my early college days. One day I walked in for my usual "donation," but the nurse gave me the fish-eye then looked at my folder with alarm, and I thought, Good Lord, they found out I'm diabetic. I thought, Holy shit, they found LSD in my blood. I thought, Sweet Jesus, they found out I'm gay--maybe the black tights, tuxedo jacket, and twenty-four-inch pearls gave me away.

II.

Besides, I *was* gay, wasn't I? So the test results were no surprise. All kinds of terrible afflictions had been promised me. I was *supposed* to catch AIDS; it was part of the plan, the price I had to pay. My father had said that AIDS was God's revenge, that my being gay was like shooting myself in the foot, that homosexuality was the same as murder or suicide in the eyes of the Lord. Hadn't Mama warned me about eyes going blind and body parts falling off?

III.

While waiting for the second blood test, I OD'd at a three-keg pool party. My girlfriend had tired of my perpetual mid-party pass-outs, so she ordered me to do a handful of speed. I did two, then two more. Within an hour, I fell into a fit of convulsions, my eyes froze open, the pool party cleared, and two ambulances and a fire truck followed the final two rounds of speed. I was surrounded by men in uniform when I heard her say, "I have no idea what happened. We were just sitting here talking when he fell on the floor and started choking on his tongue." She said it so casually; it was like she was describing a glass shaken off the counter by a mysterious vibration.

IV.

My parents each made the sign of the Cross when the therapist announced there was nothing wrong with me, nothing a few cures wouldn't fix. I wasn't gay, not really. It was an illusion or delusion, like the false positive of the HIV test. All I had to do was to stop wearing black eyeliner and rosary beads, to give up the tube skirts and tuxedo jackets. I had to read the sports pages and memorize game scores. Stop dying my hair magenta and listening to the Sisters of Mercy. Change your behavior, he said, and you change.

V.

When I reached San Francisco, I found the wild-eyed riot I had been looking for. First ACT-UP, then Queer Nation and an explosion of gay clubs in the SOMA warehouse district. Ecstasy and house music crashed down on the city like a white tidal wave. In the Gold Room at Colossus, a sea of hands rose to the ceiling over a crest of white crew-neck T-shirts. In the main room, a twenty-foot-high stack of speakers pumped out the crackling anthem of the moment. "Everybody's free," the song said. Then another threw down the challenge, "Are you ready to fly?"

VI.

I was fumbling through words, trying to describe how long it had been, how little I'd tried, when he put a finger to my lips and said that all my talk was turning him on. He wanted to take me home and show me everything. How to stroke and bite his nipple, how to lick the curve of his underarm. How to press the spot between his legs to delay an orgasm. How to put on a condom without losing the heat of the moment. How to enter him from behind, from the side, from on top. How to spread my own legs and rock under him. How to find a rhythm and how to hold it with a really long kiss. How to keep my eyes open and let my skin catch fire.

VII.

He had gotten high on smack and swallowed some guy's come in the back of a bar. Instead of nodding sympathetically, I burst into a near-rage, "How could you?" I demanded, "How could you forget about everything you taught me?"

But when I saw his eyes sink back in his head, I forgot my fury and kissed him on the lips. "It's all right," I said, "Just be careful, baby. Be careful." I really meant "Be safe." Less than six months later, he tested positive for HIV and my heart sank. I had been too hard on him. I hadn't said the right thing. I hadn't saved him.

VIII.

A charge ran through my body as I thought, this is it, this is what all the excitement was about, this is what it feels like to fuck a guy without a condom. My legs and his legs locked together and my eyes shut down on a dream: I was in a tent near a bayou in Louisiana and I could hear water running nearby. I was safe, safe in a tent with a boy squirming under me. I put my lips to his mouth and let my tongue find its way inside. I rocked and thrust and eased my way in and out of him until he finally flipped me over and slipped inside. Afterwards, I felt nothing, only exhaustion and the curly edges of sleep.

IX.

A friend and I sat in an East Village bar as I told him what had happened. After I got through stammering and fidgeting, he let his sharp, but quiet gaze fall down on me. Eye to eye, we stayed still and silent until he raised his hand from the table and brought it hard and fast against my face. "What the fuck were you thinking?" he said, "Have you forgotten everything?"

X.

And I realized that I had. I had forgotten the scare of the false positive test, the feeling that I was going to die. I had forgotten the marches and the banners and the sight of my roommate covered in lesions. I had forgotten my friends who had already died, Bill and Kelly and Charlie and Jeff and Malcolm and Francis and Daniel and Chris and Roger and Clinton.

Ten years passed, a decade, and I've changed that little. Or maybe I've changed so much that I've come full circle. I'll have to get tested again, and again I'll have to wait for the results. I'll sit tracing my hands over my body looking for trouble spots. Listening for a hollow murmur, a dull echo. Staring in the mirror waiting to go blind. Plucking out an eye, a black pearl.

FAIRY SONG

by Martin Pousson

The day before that long drive to the bayou, everything had already gone topsy-turvy, from too much magic or too little, from too many carnival days or too few. The winter air was balmy when there should have been a chill. There was a belt of sun when there should have been a sheet of fog. And there was a spinning fairy where there should have been a boy.

Even before the carnival, I spoke with the wrong mouth, raised the wrong hand, and wore the wrong face. But by Mardi Gras day, I lost all sense of how to behave. That's why we where headed—in silence—to the bayou, why Mama was driving me to that halfway house. Maybe there I'd learn what other boys knew as well as their names: how to walk, talk and act like a man, without a mask, without a costume of any kind. Maybe there I'd drop the fairy wings and learn how to be a real boy.

By the time I turned thirteen, my appearance caused enough trouble that my parents could hardly look at me. My beer-drinking father could raise the roof with a line of curse words, but he flinched at the sight of his son and disappeared within the walls of his own house. My bible-quoting mother could knock down doors with a line of holy scripture, but she could only see me through the clouds of the Old Testament. Both my parents turned away to avoid the disappointment of their son. Tongue-tied, limp-wristed, and bushy-haired, I was a manic little canary, a cartoon girly-boy who couldn't stop singing the show tunes of that Jewish woman in the movies.

Anytime I spoke, a nest of snakes coiled around my tongue to throw an S into nearly every word, and anytime I ran, a flock of birds lifted my hands into flapping motions. Papa threw a ball, and off I'd go, a light-footed little sissy to miss it once again. Mama ordered me to sit outside in a circle of tanks and trucks, and I'd drag my Ken doll out of hiding.

If I was caught whirling naked in my room with Ken's rubber head as a microphone, my parents didn't applaud or join me in singing the words to "My Man." Instead, they stared, unblinking, certain that I was a changeling, certain—as they put it—that I was the son of some other mother or father. Mama's eyes grew fiery, and her gospel tongue grew hot, and she told me exactly where I'd end if I didn't change back into the golden boy she'd known, when my face glowed with the promise of first grade and the shimmer of my first row of straight-As. I still won all As in school, but I couldn't catch a fish, shoot a duck or tell the difference between a doe and a buck. I couldn't catch, throw, kick or hit a ball. I couldn't click my finger against my thumb, whistle through my teeth or roll my tongue into a log. In all the ways that counted in Acadiana, I was not a real boy.

Long before that day at Mardi Gras, before I was sent to the halfway house, both my parents worried that I was flying toward a fiery furnace, both worried that I might flip into some other place, that I might end up as a twisted flapping fairy in some swampy neverland.

But, unlike my father, Mama stepped out of the clouds again and again to try to set me straight. She'd sing a low gospel song or a song about diamonds and mockingbirds and promise to make everything right. When I couldn't hammer a wood block into place, she finished the school project for me. When I couldn't stain the wood evenly, she grabbed hold of a brush to cover the blots and splotches. So if I couldn't keep the teenage worry off my skin or the girly sounds off my tongue, she'd take care of that too.

One morning after I slipped an S into every last syllable, she drove me in a heated fury to the emergency room, the Catholic one, to demand immediate surgery.

"There's something wrong with his tongue," she told the nurse, who first gave Mama the fish eye then a knowing look.

"Lisp," the nurse mouthed and pointed to me, as if the word was too terrible to say out loud.

Mama nodded and ran her hand over my head. "Don't worry, baby," she said, as if I was once again a small troubled thing in her arms. "Just leave it to Mama and the good doctor. After all, there's nothing a knife can't fix."

Once the doctor cut the extra flesh under my tongue, Mama went to work on the trouble of my face. My skin had begun to break out in hives and my constant scratching opened up sores. She tried to conceal the bumpy red spots with salves and the pale cream of her own foundation, but those spots broke out afterward with even greater fury. It's enough that I walked like a ballerina. Did I have to look like a moon-cursed girl? Did I have to chew my nails, bite my skin and pull at my hair?

Mama's efforts—and her own worry—only made me more confused. I should cover every flaw with make-up, but I should not walk or talk like a girl. I should play outside with tanks and trucks, but I should not get one speck of dirt on my just-pressed trousers. Instead of growing sure of how to be a real boy, I began to feel like an imposter, that I was supposed to impersonate the movements of someone I hadn't met. More and more, I felt split in two, and neither half seemed right or real.

Mama's early watch over my body didn't turn me into a boy—or a girl—but it did make me fitful with worry. I was not just ill at ease. It's as if my own flesh was alien to me. I shed dried-up layers of skin in puffs of powdery dust, I shed strands of hair like molting feathers, and I shed my face like a plastic mask.

For as long as I thought no one was watching, I wore the face of worry, which was also, apparently, the face of a girl. Even before she forbid me to play with other boys from the street, before anything at all happened with the neighbor's son, before all that, a germ of doubt irritated the spot between my eyes. At an early age, I'd stand before the mirror for long stretches, staring at the burning spot as if something was concealed there. From the start, I couldn't figure out how to be the little man Mama wanted. I couldn't figure out which face to wear.

The early pictures don't agree. In fact, they conflict with the story. In some of those pictures, I look like a budding quarterback, like a miniature husky athlete, ready to catch a football, a debutante, or a Mardi Gras doubloon, whichever was tossed my way first. With a jutting chin, jug ears, and a lusty grin, I look like a prairie Cajun, like a blue-eyed cherub. I look as if I might strap a washboard on my chest and tap out the beat for a fais-do-do, as if I could choke back a beer even in the middle of a storm. I look, in other words, a lot like my father's son.

But the image is false. In the mirror of my father's eyes, I merely reflected the appearance of a man I'd never be and a history I'd never continue. Sure, a tiny idea flickered for a while, a bright-eyed boy, a brawny and brash little man, bien dans sa peau, as his own father would put it. The idea, though, is just as false as the image. In those early pictures, I beamed, but the light was only a reflection, and, as soon as Papa's face turned, the world around me would go dark again.

In later pictures, I look glum. Worry is suspended around my face in a low-lying cloud. I look less like the football star and more like the moon-faced debutante, the one who fell under the bright lights right as her name was announced. That hand propped under the chin looks suspiciously weak. Those eyes look not just vulnerable but vanquished. And the mouth is drawn into a wobbly line.

There were other faces I wore, a whole closet full of ornate masks. In that closet, there were long twisted bird beaks and dark shadowy eyes but also bright candy-colored cheeks and huge, spinning pupils. With my changing faces, I was ready for mass and the somber pageantry of the French Catholic church. I was also ready for carnival and all the joyful terror of Mardi Gras.

If there'd been a Mardi Gras fable, the topsy-turvy carnival might've made some kind of sense. Of course, Mardi Gras was not supposed to make sense at all, not supposed to mean one thing or another. But try telling that to the masked thirteen year-old boy who watched on that day as men hollered at his mother, as men pawed at the patchwork satin of her fairy tale costume. Walking through the carnival streets of our little town, I quickly learned that Mama's face changed colors too. Her green eyes, always open, always alert when staring in my direction, shuttered and fluttered before the crowd of men. The black satin mask perched on her nose seemed to reveal more than it concealed, as a rush of excitement darkened her lips and parted them again and again in a bright little gasp. She was the center of the world, this Cajun woman, and I wanted the face she wore.

All the men's faces seemed distorted to me, twisted up in purple, green, and gold, all the gaudy colors of popsicles and all the greasy sheen of blood sausage. But those faces didn't only frighten me. They also thrilled me into laughter, and I felt the urge to point. Here was a loud-mouthed pelican, with a bent beak and mangy feathers. Here was a green-nosed alligator, with glowing eyes and a row of shimmering triangles on his back. Here was a hairy-faced wolf with low-hanging shorts and moss-covered arms. I wanted to touch each one, to sniff the gamey musk of monster after monster, but their hands passed over me to reach for my mother, as they sniffed the taboo rose of her scent.

In the mass of men, then, I could disappear, and that alone was as thrilling as it was frightening. For a while, I was just the odd thing at my mother's side. For a while, no eyes met mine. And, for a long while,

I was all ears. All around me, I heard the dying sounds of Cajun men, the horse-throated grunts and pony-high whines of their talking songs.

When a cup of gumbo hit a man's mouth, he whinnied with gratification, as if an invisible hand had just run down the slope of his neck. When he picked up a hot link of boudin, he whistled in anticipation as if to say this would be the one, the link that would take him back to the days of the Acadian cabin, rising high on cypress piers with bousillage in the walls and a fraternity of boys in the attic. When he picked up a ruby slice of watermelon, he wet his lips like a thirsty wolf as if to say no amount of drink could quench his thirst, not even the bloody flesh of a melon. Still, he wouldn't stop trying. He'd chug back cup after cup of beer, bourbon, and any backwater hooch for a souvenir taste of the man he used to be.

Now he worked at the mill, not the farm. Now he worked in the office, not the mill. Now he drove a truck, not a tractor. Now he picked up a phone, not a plow. Now he'd forgotten the French punch line to his father's joke, the French chorus in his father's song, and now—in the middle of Mardi Gras—he watched as other men pawed at the French flower of his wife.

Every Cajun man was, in some real way, smaller than the man before him. My own shrinking father, the dwarfing giant, slunk behind my mother as the carnival men danced in the street and the tent barkers ate and drank with furious eyes. Tall Capuchin monks and medieval friars passed by on rickety hand-made floats, with twisting tassels and sequined robes in tatters. Short comic book nuns stood behind them in beaded wimples and garter belts, with balloon breasts and flaming red wigs. They passed the steeple of the Catholic church, the arch of the cattle feed store, and the altar of the recording studio where Cajun bands sawed out the uneasy beat of a waltz. They passed the bronze-plated statue of the governor whose eyes seemed to follow you no matter what direction you moved, as empty as a pair of pennies.

Like that governor, the eyes of every man wandered blankly and wildly at once. Like him, everyone wore a mask. Everyone flashed the nervous smile of a suspect. On this one day, in this one festival, everyone was someone else. The monks were camouflaged farmers, and the nuns, it turned out, were teenage boys in costume. Everyone could laugh at what they were not. Everyone could gawk at the made-up faces. But no one, not one Mardi Gras reveler in the whole town, looked straight ahead at the fact that they were dancing on a grave, marching a parade right over the dead ground of a phantom state.

No one opens a museum without a plate of fossils or a mug of bones, and no one throws a parade without a skeleton or two. Still, the figures are hairless and dead. And that's the way our Rex looked as he waved from his shoddy wicker throne. With his head cocked back and a banana leaf as a scepter, he let loose a manic laugh and shouted in French. He ruled over nothing really, just a drunken day, but he ruled nonetheless. And, before him, no man could hold onto anything, not the drink in his hand, not his wife, and certainly not the boy at his side.

Maybe I wouldn't have been sent down to the bayou if I'd behaved that day, if I hadn't taken that chance to slip out. While Mama fended off the men pawing at her, and while Papa gripped his tallboy can of beer, I pulled a disappearing act of my own when I saw the 21 year-old face of the neighbor's son, the one who moved away after the storm and after we were caught, or almost caught, in the act.

Now, he stood in the middle of the crowd with a rubber bat dangling from his ear and a top hat, a white cane, and a black cape draped around his back. Half the hat was crumbled and half the cape torn, and his teeth were oversized for his mouth. Except for the bat, he was the picture of some two-faced cleft-chinned horror movie villain, and I was filled with the heat of envie all over again.

Before his family moved from our block, the neighbor's son had left me his comic books—the ones he owed me and more—and he left me with a burning want. At first, I'd been a five-year old hustler, accepting the prize of those comics for the dirty business in his bedroom. Soon, though, I wanted not the comics but the long rope of his arms and the force of his touch. The last time I let him lie on top of me, there was a rumble outside his door, and I was sure someone, his father or mother, had been listening. I was sure that I heard a phone dialing out afterward. At least, some sound rang and rang in my ear. Without anyone saying so, I knew what we were doing was wrong, knew exactly where it would lead, but I didn't want it to stop.

And now, in the middle of Mardi Gras, I wanted it to start all over. I wanted his dark sunglasses to pass over my face and for him to pin down my arms again. I saw us on the ferris wheel, on the rollercoaster, onstage holding hands with a pair of beaded crowns on our heads. And as I saw all this, I began to flap my hands like a girl and to dance around in a jittery circle as if I had a burning need to unzip my fly and let loose with a fitful piss.

Of course, he didn't recognize me. I was just five back then and wore a different face now. He didn't even look in my direction.

But Papa must've recognized the neighbor's son when he found me. He must've recognized my flapping arms and the vapor coming off my skin. And he must've heard the commotion when that name hit the air.

"Fairy," someone said, "Just look at that fucking fairy."

Suddenly, my tongue fell out of my mouth, and I hit the ground with the feather-weight force of a dizzy carnival queen. My head throbbed against the hard ground, and my nose stung as it filled with blood. It was one thing to the wear the face of a fairy and another to be called one in the middle of a crowd. Even during carnival, even when everyone was in costume, people could still tell a real boy from a fairy. A man might turn into a lady—for a day—and a lady might turn into a man. But a boy who was forever something in between, that was another story.

Papa didn't say a word—he hardly ever did now—but through the swampy fog of beer and boudin, he stared me down then threaded his hand in a chain with mine before dragging me back to the festival stage to face my mother. It was not enough that I dressed like Tinker Bell at Mardi Gras, with glittery wings and a baton as a scepter, it was not enough that I lisped and twirled in front of everyone in the street, I had to go mooning after the old neighbor's son too. I had to shame the whole family with the fiery glow of my envie.

When I stood before Mama, she saw the tattered costume and the blood running down my nose, but she didn't pass out or scream. Instead, she recognized the sign and saw the cure.

The next morning, she packed the car for the trip to that halfway house on the bayou, where there were other boys my age who hunted and fished and ran wild in the woods. There, she announced, this fairy would learn a real lesson. There, in the sizzling heat of the sun, my feathers would melt and my costume would burn. That was what she saw.

But she didn't see the rest of the story. Once my costume burned, I'd run shirtless with a dozen other boys through the woods. With my wings gone, I'd flap my arms even more furiously. In the end, I'd land in an upside-down place, forever flipped, with both eyes shining like empty mirrors.

Each of those twelve boys would suddenly see the use for a fairy. Each of them wanted some kind of satisfaction. So I'd open my mouth to sing a fairy song. I'd blow each one. I'd be the fucking fairy.

In return, they'd deliver a hard punch to my chest, a hard jab near my eye, a stinging glob of spit. They'd break open my skin and give me the true face of a real boy.

In my ear, now, their voices still rise and fall, rise and fall.

Isn't this the lesson? Let one thing turn into another, and the whole world goes topsy-turvy. Let it happen, let one carnival fairy loose, and every man breaks into a terrible song.

SHANE ROOKS

I paint (super) heroes. My Flying Flags are meant to capture many things, one of which is the freedom of a body seemingly unencumbered by gravity. I chose the image of a flag dancer because to me, he is emblematic of the sense of celebration, optimism and joy which the gay community embodies at its best. This joy is a thing I deeply love in the gay community. To me, it is that lift that carries us over the challenges we face to our families, our liberty and our health.

▼

Flying Flags 1
by Shane Rooks

FLYING FLAGS 2
by Shane Rooks

FLYING FLAGS 3
by Shane Rooks

KEVIN SKIENA

Kevin Skiena is the 2004-05 recipient of the Eugene Van Buren Prize for fiction and a winner of the 2004 A. E. Hotchner Playwriting Competition for the full-length play Post Departure. In 2006 he received his MFA in fiction writing from the University of Washington. His work has appeared in Hayden's Ferry Review. He currently lives in Seattle.

▼

IMPRINTS
by Kevin Skiena

I deserve this, Peter thought. *The body betrays us,* he thought. In a bathroom stall at three in the afternoon, under pale, buzzing fluorescent lights, he twisted his penis between his fingers to get a better look, thinking, *The past writes itself on us with X-acto knives.*

Back at his desk it was all he could think about, the small red bump on the shaft just below the head. It itched, but not badly. It burned, but not badly. Still, among all the signals wired to his brain it was the only one that had a megaphone, and it told him in a loud, booming voice that no one would love him again, not ever. He opened a new email window, addressed it to Mark, and closed it.

"Peter." Howard stood over his desk and rested an arm on a filing cabinet. "Lucy's out again tomorrow. She just called."

Three days in a row.

"We're still looking at a Wednesday deadline. You gonna be all right?"

"Sure."

Howard smiled, an uncle's smile, and patted Peter on the shoulder.

Peter worked, checked email, forced pleasure and ease into conversations in which he felt neither. What he felt was fragile, delicate. He felt like a dandelion in an open field losing more of itself to the passing breeze. He felt like a cold glass in a hot room. In the kitchen, Sandy started talking to him about a television show they both watched. Peter had missed this week's episode for a third date with José and hadn't yet caught up, so Sandy talked about the *feeling* of watching it, the *excitement* and *satisfaction,* and Peter's attention fell away and found itself sifting through memories of six weeks ago. Mark across the room at Purr. Then again a few hours later at The Cuff. The breakup had been three months before. "You look good," Mark had said, touching Peter's arm. "It's good to see you." A drink or two later and they were on the patio, their legs touching, fingers punctuating the conversation on the other's chest and shoulders. As Peter fumbled with the keys outside of his apartment Mark kissed the back of his neck. Peter knew then that this did not mean they would start again, that this was, in some ways, a mistake, but he did not yet know how big, and for the moment it was like one of those dreams he used to have, of being together again, only to wake up alone and miserable, the work of remaking himself somehow having reset itself.

By five he could hardly think straight. Everyone was going out for happy hour, but Peter said he was tired. At home he went into the bedroom, closed the blinds, and examined himself under the bedside lamp. In the calm and peace of his bedroom it looked more pink than red, more dry than sore, and for the first time it occurred to Peter that it might be nothing, a benign skin condition with a bizarrely long and empty Latin name. His mind hinted at relief. Imminent death was, for the moment, off the table. He went to the bathroom for a dab of Vaseline and changed into a softer pair of briefs.

By morning his brain had been washed clean of it. He showered, shaved, ate breakfast at the kitchen counter while listening to the radio. There was minor flooding outside the city. There was a growing state budget deficit. A dog had awakened its owner during a fire. All of it was very common, very reassuring. His mind began on the day's events. With Lucy out he would need to go to Records & Archives himself. He would need to consult with Marketing about graphics, and he would want to make sure his sales projections were still accurate. He dreaded the work to come. He dreaded another day of slogging through old budgets and reminding himself how to use PowerPoint. He dreaded the weekend, when he should be relaxing but wouldn't, his mind still churning with things left to do, and Monday, when he'd need to spend the morning catching up Lucy. He wondered if she were truly sick.

On the downtown bus he tried to think of something to look forward to. José. Their Saturday night date. He reminded himself of the things he liked about José. José asked intimate questions, withheld judgment of the responses, and expressed himself clearly. He was strong-armed and had a sweet, singsong accent. Peter could easily imagine the possibility of sex that night, and here the memory returned. Halfway between home and work, his body still struggling awake on a crowded bus, he suddenly felt half-dressed. He had not checked it that morning. He had not applied Vaseline, did not even notice if the Vaseline had helped. Now he'd done it, he thought. Now his penis would dry out and flake off because he'd forgotten to apply Vaseline.

At work he went immediately to the bathroom. He locked the stall door and dropped his pants. The spot remained, pink and oval-shaped with a clear border, perhaps larger, perhaps the same size, certainly no better, and, a few millimeters down, a second had bloomed. Peter stared, the perfect treatment at the moment seeming to be disbelief. An hour later, sick with anxiety, he went into Howard's office.

"Howard, I'm not feeling too good."

Howard, from behind a lacquered, pine desk, with five skyscrapers and Puget Sound as a backdrop, looked at him.

"I think I should go home."

Howard took off his glasses and put his hands together.

"I think it might be a cold."

"A cold," Howard said. Peter wanted desperately to leave the room.

"It might be nothing."

"Nothing."

"Maybe I should go home."

Howard rocked back and forth. "You have been working pretty hard, Peter. A lot has fallen on your shoulders this week. It's a Friday, though. You'll have the weekend. Maybe take a couple breaks today, slow it down a bit."

"Okay."

"Try not to worry about it. Worrying only makes it worse."

"Yeah."

"If it becomes a full-blown cold, obviously, or if you feel like you need to – I can't tell you how many times I've come in on four or five hours sleep and thought I had a cold. I go home, take a nap, and kick myself for a wasted afternoon when I wake up."

"Yeah." Peter stood halfway out the office door.

"My wife takes Echinacea. She loves it. Give me a heads up if you're taking off, though. Okay?"

Peter cursed Lucy for her foresight in getting sick on Wednesday. He took his lunch at his desk, closed the door to his office, and did Google image searches of every sexually transmitted disease he could think of. He saw genital warts sprout like cauliflower from the skin. He saw blisters, weeping sores, human tongues coated thickly with white fungus. He was horrified, sick to his stomach, but searched on, scanning these things for a sign of familiarity. Suddenly it seemed to him that for all the years leading up to now he'd been lucky to have loved unscathed, unburdened by viral baggage. He'd never had to warn anyone, to couple the anticipation of sex with the dread of confession, or suffer the rejection that so often comes with it. He'd always been safe, even that last time with Mark. Still, he knew these things happened, that the possibility of getting hurt or sick would always be part of it.

Whatever he had was in the early stages, too immature to identify on his own. Like almost all adult things, he recognized that this came with responsibility, and he felt the weight of it coming over him. He called his doctor's office and made an appointment for Monday morning. He had no idea when and how he would tell José, or if they'd even make it that far, but more pressing in his mind was the realization that he'd have to call Mark. By the afternoon, resigned to these things, he actually felt better. An hour before five he went into Howard's office.

"Howard, I'm going to be late on Monday. I have a doctor's appointment."

Howard raised his pen and dropped it to the desk, sighing, and fell back in his chair. "You have the whole weekend. You don't want to wait and see how you're feeling?"

"I'll be in after lunch."

"So you're predicting you'll be better? Then honestly, Peter, what's the point?"

"Lucy's been out three days."

"And you more than anyone are aware of how hard that's been for us."

"It'll just be a few hours."

Howard stood. "It's not about the hours. It's about the . . ."

"Have you ever had something on your penis?" Peter interrupted.

Howard's eyes burst open. "I, uh . . . what?"

Peter felt the warmth of blood rushing to his face. "Thank you, Howard. See you Monday." He turned and left.

Late Saturday morning Peter twirled his cell phone around on the coffee table, flipped it open and shut, trying to decide whom to call first. He called José. They talked about their weeks. José made sympathetic noises as Peter told him about Lucy's absence and the upcoming deadline. They made plans for that night, dinner and drinks. Then Peter called Mark.

"Hey. How's it going?" Since the breakup Mark's tone on the phone was always of complete indifference.

"Fine. There's something I need to talk to you about."

"Okay."

"Are you free?"

"You mean in person?"

Peter scratched his neck. "Yeah."

"Um, I'm pretty busy this weekend."

"It won't take long. A half hour. Tomorrow?"

"I can't tomorrow."

There was a pause. Peter heard street sounds and people talking.

"Are you all right?" Mark asked, concern entering his voice.

"I'm fine," Peter said. "What about this afternoon?"

"Is three okay?"

"Yes."

"Okay."

Peter arrived early and sat outside a coffee shop on Broadway. Mark arrived a few minutes later carrying a satchel and a shopping bag, a light sweat on him from the walk, They hugged and sat. Peter told him everything, pausing whenever someone passed.

"How do you feel," Mark asked when he'd finished.

"Fine. Tired, maybe just from worry."

"When's your appointment?"

"Monday. Ten-thirty."

Mark was silent for a moment. "I don't know what to say."

"You were the last person I was with. I wasn't with anyone between us and that night. It's been only you for a year and a half."

"Yeah."

"And at my last physical I was clean."

Mark sat back. "Okay."

"Are you having any symptoms? Anything like this?"

"No."

Peter took a breath. "Was there anyone else?"

"Does it matter?"

Just say it, Peter thought. "Yes."

"Yeah," he said.

Peter felt himself falling away. "When?"

"After the breakup."

"Was he clean?"

"Yes."

"You tested him yourself?"

Mark rolled his eyes.

"How do you know?"

"Because he told me. I asked him."

"And you trust him? Who was he?" As soon as he asked Peter saw that it had been someone he knew, someone they both knew.

"We were safe. Completely," Mark said.

The air was crisp. Peter felt it sting his eyes. "Not completely."

"What are you, Catholic? We were safe."

"Did you blow this guy?"

Mark stared.

"And you blew me. You fucking came home with me."

Mark lowered his head. Peter watched him, believing himself wronged, believing himself the victim. He was owed something and he would never get it. This meeting had been a mistake. An email would have done the job. *I have this. Get checked. You're an asshole.* Instead he'd chosen this. Why? He knew why. It was for the same reason his brain fed him those dreams months ago, the same reason he'd kept an eye out for Mark while running errands or at the clubs. The pieces of yourself that attach to someone in a relationship get torn away when they leave. Another encounter brings the hope of restoration, of reconciliation, but of course the thing is broken. The pieces have scarred over, and when they brush against their missing parts the only sensations that come are raw and sensitive. How long did this take to learn?

"Okay," Peter said as he stood. "Now you know. Tell your friends. It makes for a good story."

"I'm sorry." Peter started to walk off. "Call me after on Monday," Mark yelled. "Will you call?"

But Peter was already at the corner, a little more of himself gone.

The tables at Bleu Bistro were shrouded by curtains and hidden in alcoves. All Peter could see of the other diners were fragments – a candlelit forearm, darkly crossed legs. The waitresses traveled between these spaces as the only emissaries, and the whole thing made Peter feel strangely lonely for who he was with.

"Sometimes I think of what I gave up, what else I could have done." José was talking about his job as a social worker. "I was good at math and science. I could have worked with computers."

"Or been a doctor."

He shook his head. "I don't think so. You see inside too many people and they stop being people."

Peter laughed.

"What?"

"I think you just described the problem with most of my doctors."

"You have a lot of doctors?"

"No," he said. "Not enough."

José smiled. "With this I feel like a part of their lives. I feel like something they need. Some of them take it for granted, but not everyone. I worked at an assisted-living home for a while, and they don't get better. They have moments, but every day they have fewer of them, and they don't get younger. But you see what you do for them. You see how you help them, how things are easier when you're there, for them, for their families. When it's good that is what it's like."

"Wow," Peter said, feeling inadequate. "You're such a good person."

José shrugged. "I'm patient and I like the work." Peter noticed their legs were touching beneath the table. "You?" José asked.

"I'm making money and collecting ulcers until I can't take it anymore."

"When will that be?"

"I don't know. I think people either fulfill their own dreams or make money fulfilling someone else's. I'm not sure what I want yet, and this works in the meantime, but I haven't given up. You can see it in the face of someone who's given up. I won't let that happen."

They sat a few seconds more, staring at the table, their legs together. "You want to go?" José asked.

"Yeah."

It was a little after ten as they walked down Broadway. People filled the sidewalks. It was that time when evening for the young had just started, when everything was still full of potential and plans were just starting to be realized, before it climaxed and descended into fatigue and drunkenness. There was energy and expectation in the air. Peter and José walked slowly, detoured through the park, and arrived at José's apartment. Peter followed him upstairs and kept his hands in his pockets as a mild dread crept into his desire. José unlocked his door and lit a dim lamp. Then they were in each other's arms, tasting each other's lips, hands roaming backs and sides. They fell to the bed and felt each other's weight upon them. Peter felt full and alive and scared, and when José started with his belt Peter froze and sat up.

"I'm sorry," he said. "This is a little fast for me."

"Are you all right?"

Images of two red spots and Mark flashed in Peter's mind, weights that might be with him always. "Yeah. I just – I thought I'd be ready, but my head is swimming. I need to slow down. I'm sorry." Peter refastened his belt and found his shoes. He wanted to tell José everything, for José to listen with understanding and acceptance, but it was too soon to ask this of him.

"You're leaving?" José said. "It's still early."

It was. Peter stopped, dropping his shoes. José made coffee and they sat next to each other at the kitchen table and talked. José asked if he could kiss him, and every few moments they would, one of them leaning towards the other, slower now, less urgently, more as an end in itself, and because it was as naked as they would be with each other tonight it took on a new significance for them. At one-thirty in the morning, tired and happy, excited to be at the beginning of something and afraid of the time bomb that might end it, Peter said goodnight.

Peter sat on a butcher paper-covered exam table dressed in a thin gown, crossing and uncrossing his arms, and looking at a print on the wall. It was Expressionist, a man fishing in a creek dense with foliage. There is nothing comforting about the artwork in exam rooms, he thought, but he could not decide if a blank wall would be worse.

The doctor entered, a tall, skinny man in his fifties. He asked Peter about work, about family, and then got to business. The last sexual encounter had been seven weeks before. Oral? Yes. Anal? Yes. Condoms? Yes. For the oral sex as well? No. "I won't lecture you," the doctor said. "Oral sex is certainly not as risky as intercourse. I read an article once encouraging the use of latex gloves for manual stimulation." The doctor rolled his eyes as he said this, and Peter felt more comfortable than he had in days. "Let's take a look," the doctor said.

Peter focused on the fisherman print as the doctor leaned in. He felt himself being twisted and pulled, the skin stretched taut between gloved fingers. "If one is fine and ten is unbearable what's the irritation?"

"Two or three," Peter said.

"It's a little dry. You try anything?"

"Vaseline."

"Nothing?"

"No."

The doctor sat up, slipped his gloves off, and washed his hands at the sink. "You can get dressed." He scribbled in the chart, then looked Peter squarely in the face.

"Psoriasis."

"Psoriasis," Peter repeated.

"It's a common skin condition. Inflammation. We treat it with a steroid. Ointment."

"Psoriasis."

"It's not contagious. It has genetic links, but it's one of those things that a lot of people have and we don't precisely know what causes it. Have you been under an unusual amount of stress lately?"

"Um."

"That'll do it. It'll come and go, maybe more so as you get older. It's nothing to worry about." He wrote a prescription. "Use that once a day for a week or two."

Peter felt as though he'd cheated something. "It's not herpes. Or syphilis."

The doctor shook his head.

"How do you know?"

"The look of it. It's possible that it could be, but based on your behavior, your symptoms, and the way it looks the odds are very small. If it'll put your mind at ease we can do a screen."

Peter stepped out into the sun in front of his doctor's office feeling relieved and tired. All that worry, all that energy gone into prepping himself for a life of contagion and caution. He knew he had cheated something, if only partially.

"Peter."

He turned to see Mark sitting at the bus stop, squinting into the sunlight.

"What are you doing here?"

"I took a gamble that you still had the same doctor. Also that you wouldn't call."

"I would have called."

"You want to get coffee or something?"

Peter felt that Mark did not, in fact, want to get coffee. "I should get back to work," he said. "I'm fine. It's a skin thing."

Mark looked relieved. "Thank god."

"Yeah."

"So you don't want to get coffee?"

"No. Thanks."

Peter looked at him trying to remember the feeling of seeing him for the first time, or the first time he knew he loved him. He could remember these feelings only by the breadcrumbs they left on the way to how he felt now. The people they had been with each other were gone, and in their places were these two, who would forever feel awkward and out of place around the other for knowing the height of their relationship had been reached. "I'm sorry about Saturday," Peter said. "I was tired and frustrated."

"Don't worry about it."

They hugged. Peter felt Mark kiss him on the cheek and reacted quickly to do the same before they let go, and they said goodbye, leaving in separate directions. Peter felt Mark's presence at his back as he walked away, knowing that eventually one of them would turn and be out of sight. He wondered if he'd be able to tell when without looking.

CHRISTOPHER SODEN

Christopher Stephen Soden is a writer, teacher, critic, lecturer and performer. He served as Director, President, Board Member and President Emeritus of The Dallas Poets Community for over fifteen years. Christopher received his MFA in Writing (Poetry) from VCFA in January 2005. His honors include: Distinguished Poets of Dallas, Poetry Society of America's Poetry in Motion Series and The LSU Outworks Festival. His work has appeared in : Sentence, Borderlands, Off the Rocks, The James White Review, Velvet Mafia, Gertrude, Poetic Voices Without Borders 2, Gents, Bad Boys and Barbarians, Windy City Times, ArLiJo, Best Texas Writing 2.

▾

SPRITE
by Christopher Soden

men arrive with clappers
dangling
like great cow bells
and from that moment
the clanging follows

us like a jilted spaniel
somber
notes tolling
from steeples
to announce us
and signal
our departure

i have learned
to jingle
like sleigh music
bouncing
on a brittle winter gust

caper with naiads
and wood nymphs
play cards
with elves perch
on the shoulders
of souls resigned
to rove and linger

wash in comet tails
forge rainbow armor
for shad and crappie
brash spirit
of air prince
of cyclones weaver
of snowflakes

i weigh less
than a sigh
or a daydream
in late april don't care
if i'm *light*
in the loafers

manhood never intended
to be weapon or tether
or measuring stick
anchor
for perpetual gravitas

let it be a wand
metronome for jigs
and reels jangling
source of merriment
tipsy and sublime

MANIFESTATION
by Christopher Soden

I am the immediate fact and instance of myself
as a man, apparent or essential, reed and reed
music (trembling from gift of wind) somber or
rhapsodic, net effect of pendulous genitalia,
hood of peter, pleated shaft, testicle bells,
blossom of father gift, usher gift, y to x,
son being arbitrary transmission of lover,
luck of Cupid's draw, swing of hammer.
I am the step again, again, of surname,
on a ladder woven by my father, Jim,
and his before him, and his before, and his
before him, Where was I before I was and
where will I be when I'm not? I am the male
cut into air, the arm reaching through

the space around me everywhere I step,
furry leg pounding the earth in despair,
in rancor, kicking up for pairing times,
reaping times, nuptial times, leaving times.
I am male choice and must choose from
acts of men before me, acting as I act,
sum of my actions in the equation
of males who've come and will follow after,
caught in that cage of expectation
from males and the others who are not.
I am the male dripping seed, mixing spit mixing
sweat mixing hurt and succor through blow jobs
and hand jobs and from behind and up against
and kisses and caresses and licks and friction.
I am the man sharing shower space with other
guys, lathering pissing singing jostling lapsing
gas in a boisterous chorus of ducks
and lions and operatic tenors and baritones.

I am the man who must know who must know

the texture of his spirit, the ripples of his
impact, dropped into the river we trouble,
scuffling somewhere between seraphim and our
last father first father father before father.
I am the man who yearns for a way back
to himself and actual wings, and so pulls
other men up close to taste and see
who I am as it comes back in recognition,
reflection, or mocks the rhythm of breeding.
I am the man who gasps and sobs and guffaws
and counts off the moments in smoke ends,
songs and jokes. I am the man who lets go.

MY KINGDOM IS FAR AWAY
by Christopher Soden

And though I cannot hear
the notes of my songbird,
or glimpse his plumage,
I will not forget the sanctity

of my birth. I do not
expect to be honored
here, though the God
who harvested your stars
plucked mine as well.

Forgive me if I find
some of your subjects slow,
my passions confound them
somehow, repulse them,
as if they had found a child
raiding the sugar bowl.

As if they cannot understand
that sweet is sweet.
If you could only smell the dark
blossoms of my country,
taste the fruits of our orchards,

I would name them for you,
weave them into the great tent
of our history. It is always easy
to mock another's customs,
paths that terrify or astonish.

While I am supposed to believe
that casting salt or imbibing
ersatz blood or the cloaking
of brides are the practices
of an enlightened culture.

I would not presume to instruct
you on the care of outcasts,
only suggest a country's values
are reflected in the treatment
of its prisoners. You cannot imagine

how I miss my home.
my groom. Even now
he is filling the basin
with hot water and lather.
He is daubing his temples

with a rich, delectable salve.
He is singing my name,
to the weary sun.
He is asking the sovereign
of all worlds
for my safe return.

WHAT I CANNOT SHOW YOU
by Christopher Soden

There are two men in the photograph.
If not the same age they are very close.
Their voices have dropped in pitch.
Scales of manhood try fugues

and nocturnes on their bobbing throats.
There are two men in the photograph.
Maybe it appears in a magazine,
newspaper, or on a website.

Perhaps it stretches seamlessly
on a billboard you pass
on your way home from work.
Sparkles from your television.

Perhaps it dozes in a shoebox.
There are two men in the photograph.
They share an attachment. You can guess
the nature of it but you might be wrong.

There are all kinds of attachment
and all kinds of men. They do not touch
but that is only a clue if they understand
they're being watched. And maybe this

is the moment just before. I cannot show
you what they might do when the sun
recedes. When liquor makes their blood
tick moment by gorgeous moment

down to the last follicle tip. When they
take an extra second to learn
about the other as they change
for a swim in the glimmering

eventide of late July. There are two men
in the photograph. We do not know what
they want. Maybe to try everything
together they've never done. Maybe just

another green and geeky hoptoad to jostle
when insufficiency swallows them
like locusts. Maybe a taproot to Spring.
I cannot show you the skittish

glee of two men no longer afraid
to merge in the salty nook of trust
and discovery. Tingle of wishes
revered. No longer afraid of the flocks

that despise their own unthinkable
cravings. You might say it is The Great
Queer Lie: what any two men might
create, given opportunity and privilege

of irrevocable gender. Glorious prickle
of whisker against whisker, testicle sac,
crevasse. Sweet leakage mingling.

JAN STARY

Jan Stary, a former diplomat, is a successful art photographer and graphic designer of the Czech origin, currently residing in Seattle, WA. He also holds a Ph.D. degree in English and Czech Philologies from Charles University in Prague, and he taught at UW in Seattle as a Fulbright Professor between 1991-1993. Jan has shown his art in many galleries both in the U.S. and overseas. In the fall, he will teach again classes in photography and political science to ECES international students at Charles University in Prague, Czech Republic. Jan's website is at www.rockheart.com

▼

QUEEN OF NARCISSISM
by Jan Stary

HAUNTED HOTEL
by Jan Stary

MARIE ANTOINETTE
by Jan Stary

PERFECT BALANCE
by Jan Stary

MAINSTREET
by Jan Stary

ROGER WEAVER

Roger Weaver's poems have appeared in The Massachusetts Review, The North American Review, Hubbub, The Greenfield Review, and elsewhere. The author of five books of poetry, his latest is The Ladder of Desire, published by the Pygmy Forest Press in 2006. Retired from Oregon State University where he taught poetry writing, he now enjoys volunteering in a local elementary school.

▼

A Seasonal
by Roger Weaver

When at last the iris is gone
and roses assume the form of beauty,
soon Summer recalls its short story.
Fall reads its text leaf by leaf,
and the bare branch locks in its core
December's grief. Just so
when you are gone,
the hand remembers, pore by pore.

My Uncle's Geranium's
by Roger Weaver

wintered over in his bedroom,
their trunks thick as saplings
in that remote ranch house.
He was different, like me
somehow in ways he came
to teach me, inviting me
to sleep in his bedroom,
a winter-dormant geranium,
awaiting the touch of Spring.
Once he laid his hand
on my thigh, asked me to trim
his nails. Clipper handy, I bent
my head to the task, pretended
not to notice his smile as his hand
stayed there. Over time's ripening
I've come to put words to that act,
affirming words telling me
I was all right just as I was,
part of his family and "family."
He was the only one who knew
how much I needed a relative like him.
Now nearing the age he left us,
I know peace because of him,
that handsome blue-eyed man
who knew what he wanted and liked,
when to keep silent, when to speak
with his hands.

About Gay City Health Project

Gay City Health Project has been providing innovative, community-driven HIV prevention and health promotion initiatives since 1995. Born out of the Gay Men's AIDS Prevention Task force in the early 90's, Gay City has been the product of collaboration between public health agencies and community activists. *Our mission is to promote the health of gay and bisexual men and prevent HIV transmission by building community, fostering communication, and nurturing self-esteem.*

Gay City is regarded nationally and internationally as a leader in prevention messaging and programming that is frank, bold, and reflective of contemporary gay culture. Blending community development, grassroots organizing, health education and advocacy with direct services, we have created programming that engages the community and empowers gay and bisexual men, including trans guys, to invest in being healthy.

Our success is born out of taking realistic approaches to health issues, and allowing members of our community to provide direction on each initiative. This approach is designed to result in sustainable and long-term change, and is based in behavioral theories of adult learning, diffusion of innovation, risk education, social marketing and empowerment.

To volunteer or learn more about Gay City, visit us on the Web at *GayCity.Org.*

2008 Program Highlights

- **HIV and Syphilis Testing and Counseling.** In 2008 Gay City served more people than ever before with its HIV Testing and Counseling program. We provided more than 2,100 tests, a 15% increase over 2007. Upwards of 40% of these testing clients report having no health insurance and are without alternative access to these services. Gay City continues to reach those at greatest risk for HIV infection. Our number of Latino clients increased by 20% in the past year, and our number of African-American clients increased as well. In 2008, we identified nearly twice as many new HIV infections as compared to 2007 and connected these men to the health resources they need to stay healthy and feel supported in our community.

Our 2008 HIV/STD Testing and Counseling partners included Seattle-King County Public Health, People of Color Against AIDS Network (POCAAN), Sea Mar Community Health, Casa Latina, the Mexican Consulate, and South Seattle Community College.

- **SHIFT: A Peer Recovery Network.** 2008 saw the launch of SHIFT: A Peer Recovery Network, this collaborative initiative enhances and extends the network of support available to LGBT individuals in recovery. As our contribution to SHIFT, Gay City organized 27 separate drug and alcohol-free events which drew hundreds of participants. SHIFT events included movie nights, a Pride dance party, a hoedown, spoken word performances, a Thanksgiving dinner, a winter retreat and many more.

Our SHIFT partners include Multifaith Works, Seattle Counseling Service and Dunshee House.

- **Gay City TV.** Gay City TV was another major programmatic launch in 2008. GCTV is an innovative, digital, multi-media project designed to foster dialogue and build community among gay, bi and trans men. GCTV records in-depth interviews with GBT men and creates short films with local filmmakers. Interviews and films are screened at local venues, followed by community discussions and posted to GCTV's own YouTube channel. One of our films has even been chosen for the New York Lesbian and Gay Film Festival!

Our Gay City TV partners include Seattle-King County Public Health, Three Dollar Bill Cinema, and local filmmakers.

OTHER GAY CITY PROGRAMS

SMOKING IS SO GAY.
JUST THE WAY THEY WANT IT.

Tobacco companies support LGBT events, bars, fairs, and media. We repay them by being 50% to 200% more likely to be smokers than the general public.

Ready to Quit? We offer FREE smoking cessation support in a queer environment! Out to Quit workshops start this month. To participate, contact Robert at 206.388.1704 or email robert@gaycity.org.

gay city

1-800-QUIT NOW

- Our **Out to Quit Tobacco Program** uses a social justice framework to address tobacco-related health disparities among LGBT people in Washington State. Our work includes smoking cessation classes, support groups, trainings, and social marketing. In 2007 our evaluation of Out to Quit showed that three-quarters of our participants were still smoke-free six months after the program!

- **Speed, Sex and Sanity** uses the arts and public dialogue to examine the relationship gay men have to crystal meth.

- **Chat Room** is a group of smaller, intimate events hosted in our very own Kaladi Brothers Coffee Shop. Gay City's staff facilitates these discussions where we talk about anything and everything affecting queer men.

- **Gay City Forums** are larger, community venues that address a diverse set of topics including: dating, sex, gay history, sexual health, spirituality, and politics. Through these forums, Gay City aims to inspire community dialogue, debate, and personal action.

- **Gay City University** is a one-day educational event of growth and learning for gay, bi and trans men. GCU offers a broad range of range of classes on subjects like health, finance, relationships, sexuality, and community.

- **Gay City Crew** is Gay City's all-ages volunteer group that is committed to creating fun volunteer activities, cross-generational discussions, and community building events. Gay City Crew events have included Movie Nights, Cook Boys Potluck, Bulk Mail Party and Yoga for Men.

- Gay City also houses and staffs **Seattle's LGBT Resource and Referral Line**, connecting callers to the information and resources they need.

How You Can Help

As a community, we take care of each by volunteering our time, supporting healthy behaviors among our friends, and contributing financially to organizations like Gay City.

At times like these, it is imperative to strengthen health and wellness services for queer men and you have the power to make an impact. You have the ability to influence the health and future of the gay community by making a contribution to Gay City Health Project. Your donations ensure that everyone seeking help and support from Gay City can receive it.

You can donate online at gaycity.org, or send your tax-deductible contribution directly to:

Gay City Health Project
511 E Pike Street
Seattle, WA 98122

About the Editor
Vincent Kovar is editor-at-large for 'mo Magazine and teaches at Antioch University, the University of Phoenix and Richard Hugo House. He lives in Seattle, WA.

3202165